REUNITED

A CASEY CORT LEGAL THRILLER

AIME AUSTIN

LOS ANGELES, CALIFORNIA

ALSO BY AIME AUSTIN

REUNITED

A CASEY CORT LEGAL THRILLER

AIME AUSTIN

Reunited
Aime Austin

This edition published by
Moore Digital Media Inc.
1125 N Fairfax Avenue
Unit 46071
West Hollywood, CA 90046
www.*aimeaustin*.com

Cover Designer: Wicked Good Book Covers
Cover images © Depositphotos, Shutterstock

Reunited/Aime Austin. — 2d ed.

"Whereof what's past is prologue; what to come,
In yours and my discharge.."
— William Shakespeare, The Tempest Act 2, scene 1

1

Pietrek Cort

April 14, 2006

The phone rang. The mustard yellow fixture jangled so loudly it took me out of my Sunday morning routine. It had been mounted on the kitchen wall from the day we moved in forty-three years back. Hesitantly, I dropped the *Plain Dealer,* pretty sure that we were safe from the tornadoes that had swept across first Iowa, then Illinois last night.

I glanced down at the pictures of the storm's devastation feeling a small bit of fear that the clouds would bring the weather east. In the time it took for me to breathe in and out, I'd pushed away that fear, the same as I'd done every morning for the last forty-three years. I had a roof over my head. Food in my mouth. No one was coming to take those away from me.

Not this time.

The ring came again, louder than the last time. I promised myself right then that after Easter dinner with Casey and her new beau, I'd once and for all pull the near antique off the wall and turn down the ringer. Maybe get rid of the thing altogether. It was all cordless push-button phones these days. No one stood talking in the kitchen anymore twirling a long cord around their fingers.

"I'll get it," my wife huffed, like it was going to be a struggle to get the phone not two feet from where she was standing. I didn't say a thing from my chair across the kitchen, though. If nearly fifty years of marriage had taught me anything, it was mostly to keep quiet.

The same went for my daughter, but of course, Casey was easier. She was a second heart outside of my body. Nonetheless, she didn't want to hear half of what I had to say about her career or boyfriend choices. And I had a lot to say about both of those. I'd learned the hard way, though, to keep most of it to myself.

Turns out, after you acquire seventy-two years on this earth and all the wisdom that comes with it, there's no one to share it with. That's the tragedy of old age. Not sickness or death, but that fact that few are interested in your hard-earned knowledge. Instead, they search on the internet or go to therapists when those of us with gray hair could probably answer nearly all of life's questions—for free.

Everyone, it seemed, needed to learn things the hard way. That fact was hardly an advertisement for human evolution.

"Who could be calling on Good Friday of all days?" Birgit asked. She moved very slowly toward the ringing phone.

"Can't say." My answer was rhetorical. All my answers were rhetorical. Kept the peace all the same.

Birgit answered the phone. I guess the caller wasn't put off by her exasperated tone because whoever it was stayed on for more than a few seconds. I was about to turn to the sports section when something about my wife's face changed.

I lifted my eyebrows in question, but she didn't so much as glance in my direction. Instead, the line between her brows got deeper and deeper. My heart started racing. I half stood from my chair. The newspaper crashed to the floor in a bloom of newsprint.

"Casey?" I muttered. It had to be every parent's worst nightmare: getting a call that their child was sick or injured, or worse…dead. With Casey no more than ten miles away, somehow she'd always felt safe. But maybe her being so close had tempted fate. There were murders, rapists, and drunk drivers in Cleveland too, if less than New York, Philadelphia, or Chicago. Plus, her car was older than Methuselah, that thing was a death trap. I pierced my wife's concentration with my stare. Her head snapped in my direction.

Birgit's sharp shake of her head stopped my tragic train of thought in its tracks.

Then my wife did something I hadn't heard in a very long time. She spoke in German. I couldn't get my head around why she'd be speaking in German or who she'd be talking to for so long. There used to be tons of old-world immigrants in the parish, but most had moved far away from the city center once they'd had kids. And their kids didn't speak German or Hungarian or Polish and even if they had, they most definitely didn't come back to Cleveland once they'd grown up and moved to more suburban locations.

"Yes, Peter von Kraus is here." Birgit put her hand over the mouthpiece and pointed the yellow receiver in my direction. I stood all the way, then waded through the paper to take the phone in my hands.

Before I could get the heavy plastic to my ear, my mind almost spun out of control. Someone had died, I was sure of it. I just couldn't get a grip on who that would be. My parents—my adoptive parents—had died years before. My sister, maybe? Though she was not really my sister but the other girl they had fostered. We hadn't kept in touch. Other distant relatives…weren't mine. I couldn't think of a single reason to put the phone up to my ear. I did it anyway.

"*Deutsches Rotes Kreuz. Ist das Peter von Kraus?*" The German Red Cross. Was I Peter von Kraus?

"*Ja,*" I answered automatically in German, probably the same way my wife had moments before. When the woman on the end of the line didn't appear to hear me, I repeated my affirmation.

"I am from the tracing service in Bad Arolsen," she continued. "We help displaced persons find their families."

I looked down at my arm, my hand, the floor of the kitchen I'd walked across for the last forty-three years and shook my head. I knew exactly where my place was…is. It was here in Cleveland with Birgit and Casey and the folks from St. Ignatius.

"I'm sorry. I'm not sure you have the right number."

"Are you Peter von Kraus? Adopted by Viktor von Kraus and Ilse Heinrich von Kraus? You were known as Marek Zamojski."

The sense of belonging I'd worked to create over these last thirty, forty years evaporated like mist. Something about that name, that obviously Polish name, shook me to the core. I'd only seen it once on some documents my adopted aunt had used to help me get a passport once Birgit and I had made the decision to emigrate. But I'd never heard it spoken. That I could remember, at least.

"This is he." My German was perfect, just like I'd been taught. Because I wasn't German. I'd known that for some years, though when Casey had pressed as a child, I hadn't had an answer for questions about my Polish roots. I'd pushed her off to her mother, who would entertain her with long-winding tales about life in the German countryside during the war and after. After a while, my daughter had stopped asking questions.

At the sound of the static crackling through the phone, I focused again on the German words coming through the line.

"Your family is looking for you—"

"Someone related to Ilse Heinrich and Viktor von Kraus?" I asked, because I couldn't imagine one of them looking for me. Maybe it was someone from my aunt's family. My adoptive mother's sister, Greta, had been fond of me, a second mother, really.

"I'm sorry. Not your German foster family. Your real family."

"My real family?" I parroted, as if I hadn't understood a word she'd said, though her meaning was perfectly clear.

"Your Polish family."

"My Polish family?" I repeated her words a second time.

"Specifically, your mother, I believe. A Maria Zamojski has contacted the tracing service."

Grateful that the cord had unspooled after Casey's teenage years and had left feet of slack, I let myself fall back into my chair. I must have handed the phone to Birgit. Because when I came back to myself, it was she who got down the notepad she used for grocery lists and took notes for a long time. Eventually she hung up the phone.

Birgit didn't speak. Instead, she wiped her hands on her apron, then thrust them back into the dough she'd been kneading. She turned on the oven, covered the bowl in a towel, then moved on to the meat. She pared the filmy white membrane from the chops, then did the thing where she stood them up to make them into what would become a beautiful circle of browned meat.

I watched her clean the potatoes and peel them so efficiently it was as if they had never had peels at all. Then the pointy ends were severed from the green beans, one by one, until there was a pile a half foot high in a basket in the sink. After the meat was in the oven and the bread in the small one on the side, and after the potatoes were in a pot with a lid firmly fitted over them, my wife of forty-nine years washed and dried her hands.

She came to sit at the table, took my hands in hers, and by sheer force of personality forced me to look her in the eye. "What are you going to do, Peter? Your mother wants to meet you."

Like I could walk out of this house, zip up a jacket against the cold, and drive a few miles to her house. As if I knew my mother. Her face had been only a shadow in my dreams for so many years. I didn't dream about her at all anymore. I dreamt about Cleveland. I dreamt in English, and if not in English, then in German. Never in Polish.

"I'm going to have Easter dinner with my family. I'll keep an eye on my daughter's not-so-new boyfriend. Then I'm going to enjoy that excellent lamb that you've prepared. When I told you in nineteen fifty-eight that I would never return to East Germany or Poland, that was a promise. It's one I intend to keep."

2

"This is the crib, fo shizzle," I said as I made the left turn into my parents' driveway. When I'd straightened the car on the gravel, then glanced at Sinclair, his nose had developed a disapproving wrinkle that was often hidden by his reading glasses.

"Tallulah, we talked about this language. There's no need to do the Ebonics routine."

"No one calls me that." Sinclair was a little bit obsessed with me acting my age. I kind of thought it was because he didn't want our ten-year age difference to look like twenty. No matter how many times I told him the years between us didn't matter, he didn't hear me. Instead, he fluffed up his nearly full head of curly hair, patted his flat stomach, and stashed his glasses far from where I could see them or where he would later be able to find them.

"Lulu sounds like a kid's name," he said, not for the first time.

I had to work hard to keep from doing the eye roll he hated more than my so-called Ebonics.

"It's the nickname my family used when I was little." I left out the fact that they'd all be more than glad to call me Tallulah. We weren't much of a nickname family, but I hated Tallulah with the heat of a thousand suns.

My older brother, David, wasn't "Dave." My younger sister, Becks, used her full name—Rebecca—whenever she was home, even though I knew everyone else called her by the shortened moniker. Mom was definitely not an "Abby." There was no nickname for Saul. It was the name of a middle-aged man, which my dad had probably been since birth, cardigans and all.

"Maybe if you used your full name, they'd treat you like an adult," Sinclair said, pressing his point. He pressed *all* of his points.

"Can we not psychoanalyze all this?" I didn't want to be mentally exhausted before I walked in the door. I needed to save all of my psychic energy for dinner.

"It was my undergraduate major," he said. "Psychology at Princeton."

"Talk about the long-ago past." I couldn't help teasing him.

"It was the eighties, not the Mesozoic era," he said. I was working on a snappy comeback while I turned off the motor. But I didn't get a chance. Sinclair looked past me toward the house on my left and said, "Your parents don't do modest, do they?"

I tried not to bristle at the comment I'd heard more times than I could count since I was about eight or nine years old and people other than my parents did drop-off. No one said it out loud, but I heard a hint of anti-Semitism in every mention of my family's apparent wealth.

"They're not WASPs," I retorted. "That's the family next door. No one ever talks about their house size." Somehow it was okay for WASPs to have big houses, second houses, and German cars. But us Jews were "flashy" if we did it. It was half the reason I'd turned down the offer of a BMW for my last birthday and had taken the Rav4 instead. I was not Japanese, so what people would have said would have been an insult, not a nickname.

He sighed his concession. "Tell me who's who again."

"My mom is Abigail Rappaport. She didn't change her last name," I interjected before he could comment. Sinclair was surprisingly traditional about some things. "She runs the Cleveland Jewish Federation. My dad is Saul Mueller. He's a psychiatrist who doesn't just hand out medicine, but does talk therapy for the entire fifty-minute hour. My brother and sister are both doctors. He's got two rugrats, Noah and Leah. So yeah, super Jewey.

"My sister's pregnant. I think there was probably some kind of fertility treatment involved, but she won't say. David's wife is Rivka. She grew up in Israel. But she doesn't really talk to men outside of the family, so don't worry about her. David's the star of that show anyway.

"Rebecca's husband is somewhere in the Middle East making a billion-dollar deal. Her last name's Goldmark, by the way. Yes, I can see it in the tilt of your head. Those Goldmarks are why Ari is across the globe closing some deal. He's always closing some deal. I can't figure out how he got his sperm six and a half thousand miles away, which is why I'm still leaning toward the donor sperm/insemination theory. Not my business, though."

My car's overhead light flickered out. I was about to take a breath to give Sinclair the rest of the rundown, but my next words were interrupted by his lips pressing against mine.

Suddenly all my family foibles didn't seem that important. Instead, I fell into his kiss. His hand slipped from the back of my neck into the collar of the wool zip jacket Sinclair had picked out. I shivered when his hand pulled down the metal tab separating the little plastic teeth from each other.

The spring air tickled at my skin. The combination of cool air and hot breath practically had me panting. For all the issues anyone could have with Sinclair, they couldn't touch this one. The chemistry between us was off-the-charts scorching.

Before that chemistry burned me and I was making out in the backseat of my SUV like a sixteen-year-old, I pulled back. When I went to zip my jacket back up, my elbow hit the steering wheel, sending a sharp piercing sound into the early evening air.

I couldn't put off dinner any longer. My mom or dad, or worse the neighbors, would probably come out to check on the noise. It wasn't the kind of neighborhood where people made too many wrong turns, or honked for that matter.

"Let's go. You're a smart guy. You'll figure it out. About the rituals, though. Just follow my lead. Got it?"

"I thought you said your family wasn't religious."

"It's Passover. We're like a broken clock, observant twice a year."

"That's twice a day for the broken clock phrase," he corrected. Sometimes I wondered why he couldn't just let stuff go. It was like he always had to be right, precise, accurate. Probably the professor in him.

"You get the point. C'mon."

I ran around to the other side of the car and opened the door for Sinclair. He said that the handles on my car were complicated. It was easier opening it from the outside rather than talking him through the Toyota's finer points.

Though my heels were low, I had to grab on to Sinclair for support on the walk from the driveway to the front door. Like most of the old houses around here, the pathways were slate. The stone slabs had the most beautiful jewel tones when they were dry, but they were treacherous when wet. Three-quarters of the days in Cleveland included some kind of precipitation, so to me the stone choice seemed stupid times a thousand.

"Damned shoes," I muttered.

"Ah, the price women pay for beauty. But you do look beautiful, you know. They make your legs look wonderful."

I sort of had to agree with that. Sinclair had introduced me to the world of sex with shoes and thigh-high hose and it was hot, hotter than anything I'd done in college or in my twenties. He liked me to wear the same when we went out. It was the least I could do to please him. My usual Dr. Martens didn't leave me feeling wobbly, though. I was grateful that I made it to the portico in a single piece.

After I sucked air into my lungs, I turned the knob of the wide front door. The vestibule stood empty. The inner door to my house was shut tight. I could hear faint voices coming from far into the house, though. I looked to the right as the grandfather clock chimed nine. At least I was on time. Mom would want to have us all there after they were back from temple. From the cars in the driveway, I knew they'd made it home.

I gestured to the large metal receptacle on the left. "Leave your umbrella there."

Sinclair hesitated for a long moment. "Will it be here when we leave?"

"It's an umbrella, not the crown jewels. I'll try to make sure my family doesn't pilfer it."

"It's just that I bought it in London after visiting the *actual* crown jewels and the sky had opened up. It's not easy to get a good strong umbrella here."

"You could always leave it in my car if it's that important." It was the second time in as many minutes that I tried not to roll my eyes. If this was how it started, it was going to be a really long night.

Sinclair thought better of pissing me off and adding more stress to my life and eased his black nylon among the others. I resisted the urge to sprint for my mom's label maker.

Letting another deep breath hiss out, I opened the wide wooden door.

"Mom!" I yelled.

"In the kitchen," she called.

I slipped my fingers between Sinclair's and gripped his hand hard. I led him through first the living room, then dining room, both devoid of anyone.

My mom looked frazzled as she always did when doing family dinners. I hugged her first even though she had a box of matzo in her hands.

"Lulu, so good to see you. We've been missing each other a lot the last couple of months. Where's the boyfriend you said you were—"

Her words were cut off when she spied Sinclair behind me.

"Mom," I said into the sudden silence. "This is Sinclair."

"Does Sinclair have a last name?" That was my dad. The rest of my family, minus Rivka, had somehow wandered into the kitchen all at exactly the same time. It was creepy sit-com-like timing. I kind of wondered if they'd planned this ambush.

"Lulu!" my niece and nephew called out in near unison. Even if I wanted to use my full name permanently, I'd keep it as long as these two were small. Their little arms banded around what they could grab of my waist and thighs. I patted their curly little heads.

Ancient Legos, that had probably taken everyone on a scavenger hunt to find, quickly distracted them from the excitement of my entrance. They each took a big bucket toward the family room. I heard the sound of thousands of plastic bricks hitting the carpet and subsequent squealing followed.

"I'm Saul Mueller," my father said, extending his hand. Sinclair grabbed it firmly.

"Richard Sinclair."

"He has a first name," my mother said. "Why don't you use it?" This was directed at me.

"I didn't want my mouth full of Dick in front of my parents," I said.

"So you just threw wool and some pantyhose over your dirty mouth," David observed.

"Yep." I nodded. "Sinclair. This is my brother, David. He's a neurosurgeon," I announced, in case there was lots of oohing and ahhing to get out of the way. "Those kids were his. Where's Rivka?" I asked. I wanted to add a question about lifting the veil of her oppression, but my lecture on fundamentalism versus feminism hadn't gone over well a few years ago and would probably go over worse now.

Becks waddled into the kitchen from the powder room under the back stairs, a half smile playing around her lips. "Kosher kitchen."

"I can't believe you haven't demolished that yet. Combined both into one real kitchen," I said to my parents.

Mom's job came with all sorts of hypocrisy. The very people who would call you on your –isms in a heartbeat were the same people who nod in approval every time she brings them to the house and gives them a tour.

Mom always starts at the back door like it's a secret entrance to the bat cave. Then she shows them through the mudroom to that first kitchen with its gas oven pilot light. Purposefully, she forgets to flip the switch, leading them through a room that doesn't have much by way of electricity, then she pulls them through to the light and bright, all-granite-and-acacia kitchen we really use. Thus assured of her allegiance, they open their wallets and give to whatever campaign is at the forefront of the fundraising calendar.

David did Mom one better and married Rivka who'd grown up on a kibbutz. As if that wasn't cliché enough, now my brother's wife clung to that kitchen like a lifeline, making sure no meat and milk mix, and no *trayf* touches her children's lips.

I've always kind of wanted to make them bacon-wrapped scallops in there, but I've held myself back through sheer force of will. Didn't leave me with much impulse control with the rest of my family.

"Well, it's getting use now. I'm happy that Rivka feels comfortable in there," my mother said, not acknowledging her complicity in whipping up religious fervor in a world that needed far less of that.

"Richard, can I call you that?" my mother asked. When Sinclair nodded, she continued. "As I've heard nothing about you, why don't you tell me about yourself."

"I'm managing pro bono at Dalton Lacey. It's a natural segue from my research at Cleveland-Marshall."

"You were a law professor there?"

"For about fifteen years."

"What a long career. Were you there when Lulu was a student?"

Sinclair nodded a bit too enthusiastically. "Tallulah was one of the bright spots in my classroom."

"Was she now?" my mother asked in a way that made me wary of what was to follow. Her, "Have you dated many students?" question didn't disappoint.

"I never dated any students while I was teaching. It's a breach of ethics, not to mention that unfortunate power differential being exploited." He omitted any mention of his long and not yet terminated marriage. I didn't hurry to fill them in. There would be time enough for that later.

"And there's no power differential with you being a partner at Dalton Lacey and my daughter climbing her way up from the associate ranks? Because you are a partner, aren't you?" My mother was a feminist with a capital F.

"We're not in the same department," Sinclair said in that voice that could melt butter. "I bring years of outside experience to the firm."

"I'm sure you do. So were you ever married? Have children?"

"My daughter is in college in Tennessee. She's just wrapping up her freshman...first year there. Great little city, Nashville."

"And your daughter's mother?" My mother did verbal gymnastics for a living. Sinclair was no match.

"It's getting pretty late. Noah and Leah have to eat, right? You want me to help you set the table?" I volunteered, steering the conversation well away from Sinclair's daughter's mother. Just the thought of one Dr. Deborah Bloom gnawed at the lining in my stomach.

His complicated marriage situation would surely send my mother into a tailspin. I thrust a platter into Sinclair's hands, picked up another, and pointed the way toward the dining room.

Rivka, like a specter, had somehow slipped through the kitchen to this room and snatched everything from Sinclair and me as she was the self-proclaimed expert at holiday table setting. Everyone in this family knew I was an expert at nothing, so I let it go and pulled my boyfriend through the living room into the library while preparations were made.

I was supposed to be telling him all about handwashing and matzo breaking, but I was leaning into him instead. Need emanating from my every pore, he took the not-so-subtle hint and in a second had pushed me against the wall. One of his hands was between the buttons of my blouse, the other under my skirt. Despite the prohibition against it, I fumbled with the dimmer until we were thrust into near darkness.

Despite my outward appearance for the last dozen years, I'd been raised to be somewhat modest. Which was why my reaction to Sinclair couldn't be explained by my rational brain. Pushing aside all thoughts of impropriety, I tugged him by the tie to the couch.

Five or ten minutes later, it was all over save for the sound of our rapid breathing. Outside the door I heard my father calling my name. Like a splash of ice-cold water, his voice had me on my feet. I hauled Sinclair into the adjoining powder room where the bright light accompanied our hand-washing and clothes fixing.

Except for the occasional rumble of Sinclair's stomach, he made it through all the rituals and dinner like a champ. He didn't even flinch when David's little ones melted down after their command performance.

When we could finally really eat, I made Sinclair a plate and sat back, proud to have eased through the hard part of dinner. My parents didn't go for the low-alcohol sugary wine, so they were well and truly lubricated. Sure I was out of the woods, I relaxed. So I was surprised when my mother's brown eyes focused with laser-like precision on my boyfriend.

"Did you say when you were divorced or widowed?"

3

Casey Cort
October 9, 2006

The residential street in Lakewood was surprisingly free of parked cars. It felt like everyone in Northeastern Ohio except me had gone away for the long weekend. Fall weather in Ohio was the best of the year and many took advantage of it even if it was only a day trip to one of the Metroparks that ringed Cuyahoga County like a necklace. Maybe I should have suggested something like that for me and Miles. We weren't in the best place with me having postponed what was supposed to be our elopement. I was still engaged with no date certain for a ceremony, and I had no good reason for the delay.

I pulled the Honda to a stop and rethought, and for a moment regretted, the couch purchase. Especially after I turned off the ignition and waited for the car to shudder to a stop. Instead of living room furniture, I probably should have used the Hudson money for a down payment on a new car that stopped when I removed the key. My butt hadn't been in danger on the futon. An engine that hated to turn off was a problem that I'd ignored too long. I twisted the key in the handle and locked the door. I almost skipped the last step in the ritual, secretly hoping some criminal opportunist would take it off my hands and I'd get my few hundred from the insurance company for a down payment on a newish version.

I walked down the empty block until I found the number I'd written in my address book some three years earlier. Back when I'd been naïve and unschooled in the ways the world worked. Back when I thought this was the home of my savior. Once I located the brick building with the word "Viktoria" etched into the stone arch above the door, I pressed the buzzer for the correct apartment.

"Yes," a deep male voice answered.

"It's Casey."

"Come on up," he said before the loud buzzer replaced the sound of his voice. I yanked on the unlatched door, went through the vestibule, and opened the one behind it before the lock reengaged. I took the two flights up to the third floor, located apartment nine, and knocked.

It wasn't more than a few seconds before the wide, darkly stained door swung open. On the other side was my first fiancé, Tom Brody. He was dressed in loose satin shorts that grazed his knees and a tight-fitting maroon T, his undergraduate college name splashed across his chest in that blocky font I've never seen off a college campus.

If I'd been any other girl with any other past, I'd have readily admitted that he looked good. He was tall and broad with warm brown eyes a more innocent girl could fall into.

His dark blond hair stood up on one side as if he hadn't yet showered and tamed it. The "just rolled out of bed" look suited him like every other look suited him. That was the province of the rich.

But I was immune. So very immune. The sight of prostitutes kept in conditions worse than factory farm animals had cured me of any lingering feeling for him. Because he liked those kinds of women far more than he'd ever loved me.

I looked pointedly at his broad, square empty hands. "Do you have it?"

"What was it that you needed from me again?" His deep baritone voice rumbled through his chest. I had to work hard to keep it from setting off an answering reverberation through mine.

"Tom. Can we not play these games? Like I emailed you, I gave you my birth certificate years ago, first for the passport, then you told me you needed it for the marriage license. I need it now."

Painful memories rose up from my chest and into my throat as bitter as bile. We'd planned for a future together two different times and neither had worked out. I'd set store on that future.

Me.

Him.

Us.

A Powerhouse Couple that Cuyahoga County would fear and admire in equal measure. Beautiful babies with his looks and my brains. I'd seen it so clearly I could have touched, smelled, and tasted it.

Instead of answering, he turned and walked into the apartment. I had no choice but to follow. When I'd called the six different government offices that handled certified copies of birth certificates, they'd told me in no uncertain terms that I couldn't get a same-day reprint of the document.

I was looking at three to six weeks on one hand and maybe three to six days on the other. Neither of those would get me a passport in time for the last-minute low-cost tickets my dad had managed to secure. Of course, he and Lulu had valid passports. I couldn't say the same.

Tom lowered himself onto a huge gray sectional and patted the cushion next to him. I ignored his hand and took the last seat past the bend in the couch keeping a wide berth between us.

With appraising eyes, he looked me up and down. "Is that a ring? You engaged again? Need your birth certificate for a marriage license?"

"Tom." My voice was a sharp crack of annoyance. "Can we not do this?" I tried to keep exasperation from my tone. If today hadn't been a holiday, I'd have asked him to send it to me via overnight mail. I'd have even swallowed courier fees I couldn't afford.

If my dad, my best friend, and I were leaving on Saturday, though, I needed it bright and early Tuesday morning for the expedited passport service center. They promised a forty-eight-hour turnaround. Which meant I'd have my travel documents by Thursday, Friday at the latest, mere hours before our Saturday morning flight. There was no time for his screwing around.

"What? We dated for three years, Casey. *We* were engaged. *We* could be married right now but for you calling off our engagement. My mother had really been looking forward to planning our wedding."

"I'm sure there is no shortage of women in Cleveland who'd be happy to walk down the aisle with you. The last time I flipped open *Cleveland Magazine* you were listed among the most eligible bachelors in the tri-county area under forty."

"That magazine cramped my style."

"I'm sure it did. Kind of hard to cruise Lorain Avenue with a famous face."

He didn't deny driving along the main drag of the city's red-light district. Instead he asked, "Who's the lucky guy?"

"Miles Siegel. You met him at one of the bar association parties."

He nodded like he was a sage on a mountain, not a john on a couch. "I shoulda guessed. He was eyeing you like you were on the appetizer menu."

I recalled that uncomfortable happy hour from years ago. Miles had sat back as casual as could be while Tom had done the possessive jerk thing. Then there'd been the repeat years later with Miles doing the same to Tom. It must be a prosecutor thing. Hopefully the two would never be in the same room again. Or the same room with me at least.

"Not that it's any of your business, but it's not for that. My dad is going to Germany. He's doing the family tree thing," I said casually even though this trip was looking like it was going to be anything but casual.

"My aunt Mary loved that stuff."

"I remember," I said. And I did. It was one of the things we were supposed to tackle on our bar trip. A little sightseeing, a bit of prowling through the basements of old stone buildings, maybe the local church, looking at handwritten birth and death records. That had been my idea of heaven ten years ago. Now I wasn't at all sure I wanted to know the answers that lay behind my father's origins, much less delve into my own reticence to marry the available guy who'd proposed to me.

"You set a date?"

"For?"

"Your marriage, Casey. Congratulations, by the way. I hope it's everything that you want it to be."

I wasn't being obtuse. Not really. Being with my ex had my mind wandering all over the place, ricocheting between past and future. His weirdly passive-aggressive words caught my attention, however.

"What's that supposed to mean?"

"I want you to be happy. It's all that I've ever wanted. If I thought I could make you happy, I'd marry you in a heartbeat."

I'm embarrassed to say that my own heartbeat sped up just a little at his backhanded proposal.

"That wouldn't make me happy," I managed.

"We could still make a good team. My contacts. Your beaver-like work ethic. It's a winning combo."

"I'm not sure being compared to a rodent is complimentary."

"You know what I mean. You work hard. Harder than I ever have. You did law review. You studied all the time in law school. And even when the job thing didn't go your way, you clawed your way up the attorney ranks in Cleveland. I hear good things about you from my dad, from the other judges. From the other prosecutors even, though they're a little grudging in their compliments. No one has a bad word to say about you."

"I don't want to be anyone's beard, Tom. I want a man who loves me for me. Not for what my good reputation, diligent work ethic, and felony-free record can do for him."

"Ouch. I don't have a record, for the record."

"Just calling it like I see it."

"How I see it, Casey, is that all that lust and wanting to be together twenty-four hours a day, all that new relationship energy? That goes away. Men pick up golf or watch other men throw a ball or hit a puck on the weekends. Women have their kids, and their own friends and careers. We all fall into a companionable coupling. We could skip all the fights and disappointments that go with that transition. Go into this thing with our eyes wide open."

It sounded so reasonable I almost considered it for a second...almost.

"Isn't it that first spark? That initial fire that keeps people together when the flame lowers to a flicker. Why should I give up that passion?"

"And you have that now? That passion?" His question lasered right to the heart of my current dilemma. I kind of didn't think so. I mean Miles was interesting and cute and not half bad in bed, but with none of the heart palpitations that actors crowed about in movies. I wasn't even sure that was a real thing. I flicked my eyes away toward the lifeless street scene outside his window.

"That's what I thought, Casey. I know 'in love' and this ain't it." He lifted his fingers to air quote around in love.

"Maybe I'm all burned out on 'love,'" I air quoted back. "I thought I was in love with you. Maybe I don't know what that is anymore. Maybe I'm doing exactly what you said, but with someone else instead." I kind of wanted to slap the two hands I had over my mouth.

He'd gotten me all shook up. None of that should have come out of my mouth. I'm pretty sure it isn't what I thought. That I was settling for Miles. I huffed out a breath to clear my head. It was kind of hot in his apartment. The spring heat had caught us all by surprise.

"I'm a better fit is all I'm saying." Tom's voice the soul of equanimity.

"Because I can't testify against you in a court of law if we're married?"

"It's my Catholic upbringing." He shrugged one muscled shoulder. "I cop to the Madonna-whore complex."

"Maybe you should see a therapist for that."

"You sound like Lizzy."

"Did you love her? Were you in love with her?" I'd compared myself to *his* first fiancée. Then in light of his nighttime proclivities, I'd forgotten to be jealous of her.

It was his turn to look away.

"Let me get my lockbox."

He was up and out of the room as fast as his long legs could carry him. In a few minutes he was back, hefting a dark gray metal cube.

He plunked it on the wood floor and went to the kitchen to get his key ring. After he sifted through all the keys, he slipped one into the lock. It turned easily. Tom pulled a latch and lifted the lid.

I stood up and came closer to look over his shoulder. There were the usual items I'd expect. His own passport, its blue cover embossed with gold. What looked like insurance papers and some other documents fell like leaves when he pulled out an overstuffed folder.

One of the documents caught my eye, but I'd decided long ago that his business wasn't mine, so I turned a blind eye. I knelt picking up and stacking random papers while he flipped through others.

"Sorry. I should have looked when you emailed me. I know it's in here somewhere. I'm total crap at some things—like relationships with really good girls, but I don't lose other people's shit."

I tried not to look at my watch. I had a ton of other stuff to do to get ready. Pack. Ask my neighbors to feed my cat. Get food for Simba so they wouldn't have to. Do some initial research on where to start the search for my dad's mom. Book a rental car. This little trip to Tom's hadn't been something I wanted to do, but was the most important because everything else was moot without a passport.

"Let's split it up," I offered. I took half the stack in my hand and paged through the documents one at a time. "Nothing."

I looked at Tom and saw he was holding it in his hand. "Here you go."

I took it in hand. Checked that it was mine, because I imagine they all kind of look alike from the seventies. Casey Ann Cort. October 30, 1970. 7:08 P.M. St. John's Hospital. It had my mother's name. Father's name—Pietrek Cort. It was the same as he'd always told me.

Now I knew that to be a lie or at least only a tiny percentage of the truth. It was a little like sitting here with Tom. With my ex, lies and truth had always had an uneasy coexistence. The world always seemed to turn upside down for me. Just when I thought I knew which way was up, it went sideways. Suddenly I had a certain clarity. I met his eyes with mine.

"So you were never in love with me, were you?"

He broke our stare. "Don't look at it like that..."

"Your heart didn't beat faster when I walked into the room. You never woke up in a sweat imagining how you'd go on without me. You didn't dream of what it would be like to wait for me at the end of the aisle, me lighting up your whole world."

I had to stop. The whole thing was too depressing. We'd never been in love. At least he hadn't been. I'd examined my feelings to death years ago and didn't want to go there again. I'd thought I'd loved him. Maybe I'd loved the idea of him, the idea of what marrying him would be. Exactly what he'd said. The big house. The fancy name. Rubbing elbows with Cleveland's well-heeled. Kids who had all the advantages the world could give. They'd have passports from birth. Wouldn't be like me, in their mid-thirties before their first trip to Europe.

I shook my head, getting the fantasy under control. Because if I took Tom out and substituted Miles in, the future looked almost exactly the same, minus the statewide family influence.

It was all too much. I needed to put clothes in a suitcase. Pick out comfortable walking shoes. Buy one of those electronic navigation systems that worked around the world. Tom was my past. After today I really never had to talk to him again. It was time to firmly boot him back where he belonged, in 2004.

I was so caught up in my own thoughts that I didn't feel the strong arms come around me. The soft kiss placed at the top of my head.

Tom whispered into my hair, "Don't do it, Casey."

I pulled back only slightly, far more comfortable than I should have been. "What? Fly to Europe?"

"Don't settle. Not for me. Not for him. You deserve better."

He placed another soft kiss first on my forehead, then another on my cheeks, then another on my lips. I broke away and saw myself out.

4

Marek Zamojski
July 6, 1942

"Get inside," Mama called from the front door of our flat. I was already halfway down the stairs to my friend's front door below us.

"Mama, I want to play," I whined. "Józef just got a new bicycle. I want to go see it. He said I could even ride it. Can you get me a bicycle?"

"You need to come inside and get dressed in your Sunday clothes. I am not going to ask you again."

Fine.

Mama sounded like she might whip me if I didn't come back right at that moment.

I turned around on the steps and stomped up to the door. Ever since my papa had gone away, my mama had stopped being like she used to with smiles and laughs and tickles. I missed him too, but that didn't mean I still didn't want to run and jump and play. None of the kids were in school, so my sister was at home too. The war had ended that. Mama said the Germans were taking everything away, including many people in our town. Lots of the other children were gone.

We couldn't really go out to the park. The war had ended that too. And now friends were off-limits also. It was like the German soldiers in their stiff uniforms and shiny black boots had marched through town and taken all of the daddies and good times with them.

I was so tired of watching Mama make soup out of whatever food she could get or watching her count out złoty complaining that we didn't have as many as we used to.

All I wanted to do was have a little fun today when Józef had called up from the street on his shiny new bicycle. I shuffled as slowly as I could without Mama noticing from the front room. When I got to the bedroom door, I pushed it all the way open. My older sister, Anna, who shared the room with me was pulling up her socks and tying on her shoes. She always did what Mama asked.

"Why do we have to put on our clothes? I was planning to play with Józef today. He got a new bicycle. I think it's red."

"Where did his parents get money for a bicycle?" she asked. It was exactly the kind of question Mama would have asked if she hadn't been so cross. "His dad probably took it from one of the Jews," she said under her breath.

"I don't know. How do people get money for anything?" All I knew is that Mama or Papa took money from a drawer in the kitchen and used coins to buy bread and meat and newspapers. I'd seen Papa put złoty in sometimes but had never thought about where it had come from.

"If you hadn't noticed, there's a war. Our papa is gone. No one has money anymore. The Germans took it all."

I tried to sort out what Anna was talking about, but I didn't really understand what she was saying. All I knew was that I probably wouldn't get to play with Józef today because we had no money or because of the war. I pulled at the buttons on my short pants trying to get them to stay closed. Why were clothes so complicated to put on and take off?

"Hurry. Get on your shoes. We have to go," Mama said, coming into the room and making sweeping motions with her hands.

"Where are we going, Mama?" I asked. Maybe we were going to the river. Sometimes there was kids' stuff going on by the water. I was getting older and was no longer as afraid of the water. Mama had promised to teach me to swim when I turned five. I looked at the lines that creased her face. It didn't seem like a good time to remind her of that promise. "Where?" I asked again, because she was staring at the wall of our room and not at me.

"To the school," she answered. That squashed away all thoughts of swimming or playgrounds.

At that, I pulled up my socks and tied my shoes all the faster. When the Germans had first said that there was going to be no more school, I was very happy. Staying at home with my mama all day had seemed like a really good idea.

Anna hadn't much liked school, and I was worried that it would be as bad for me too. But watching Mama worry about Papa and how much food we didn't have wasn't any fun either. Mama no longer sang all the fun songs or sewed toys like she had before. I'd wished on so many different days that I could go to school, if only to have a break from

Mama's face creased with lines on her forehead and her eyes filled with tears when she was putting on the kettle and thought I couldn't see her face.

Now, though, I was a bit worried. Would I have to sit all day in scratchy, uncomfortable clothes? Would there be any time for playing or just learning letters and numbers? Or would there be something to do that wasn't watching my mama wringing her hands and checking the box for letters from my father? He was supposed to be working in a camp in Germany or Yugoslavia, somewhere very far from us.

But I'd heard my grandma say he was really dead, which meant he would never come back. I didn't think that was true. I pulled at my clothes again. Maybe itchy and scratchy wouldn't be so bad if I didn't have to keep an eye on my mama when she forgot to get out of bed or forgot to make us lunch. My sister's sandwiches were not good like Mama's.

Excited to see what would happen, I followed my mother out the door and skipped behind her all the way to the rainbow-colored buildings that made a huge square in the middle of the city.

When we got there, I stopped suddenly and crossed my legs to keep from wetting myself. I tried to remember that I was a big boy and past peeing in my clothes. I used the potty all the time like Mama and Anna. Mama had told me that I was too big for a diaper. I'd forgotten to go this morning, though. I had been too excited about the bicycle to remember to use the toilet. Then I'd forgotten again in my rush to get my clothes on so Mama didn't get angry. Now, I was stuck until I could find a place behind a building where no one would see me. Going outside was a secret Papa had said boys and men kept to themselves.

When we got to the square, there were German soldiers everywhere. Not the two or three that usually marched around with their shiny black boots kicking high in the air. There were more than I could count. Anna had taught me to count to twenty, and I knew I could never count as high as there were men in uniform. There were also men not in uniform, but with square German faces and blond hair that didn't move with the wind. Even though Mama combed it down with water every day, my hair always lifted up into curls. Mama said it looked like a halo in the sun like the pictures in the church windows.

Though I knew I probably shouldn't stare, I looked at all the strange men. They wore dark suits even though it was warm. They carried round black bags that bulged with stuff. One day maybe I'd grow up and be a soldier. I'd get a nice uniform and new boots and a rifle.

I would be a nice soldier who helped people who were lost and didn't yell and jab people with the end of my gun. I hadn't told Mama about my grown-up dreams. She would probably cry even though I would try to explain that I would be a nice Polish soldier, not a mean German one.

I turned to my mama. Her eyes were round with some kind of emotion that scared me. More than anything I didn't want her to cry. When tears ran down her cheeks, my throat hurt and I couldn't breathe and I ended up crying too, even though I wasn't at all sad. I tugged at her blue cotton skirt, the same color as the kerchief on her head.

"Mama, I want to go home."

My father had disappeared on a day like this. With soldiers and guns and shooting. I remember Mama screaming and Papa being pushed and dragged through the street with other men from our town. Suddenly, my heart knocked so fast I thought it would come up out of my throat and I'd choke on it.

"Hush, Marek. If you could read, you'd know the flyers said that we had to come here. On this day. At this hour. See the clock on the tower? It's almost nine."

I shielded my eyes from the sun and tried to make out the golden numbers and red hands on the dark face. It was hard for me to tell time no matter how many times Mama explained the big hand and little hand. I blinked back tears from the sun. It didn't matter anyway. My heart started up again. I grabbed tighter at Mama's skirts.

"What if they take you away?" I was starting to tremble even though I knew I shouldn't. I didn't want anything to happen to my mama even if she was sad these days. She was the person who took care of me. Grandma was too strict. If I asked for a candy, she always said no. Gave me castor oil when she was visiting us. Counted how many times I went to the bathroom. Scolded me when I didn't poo every day.

A single rifle shot into the air made all the adults and children fall silent. I didn't dare repeat my question. One of the soldiers stepped forward.

"All children," he announced, "shall go into the school building. Parents, you are to wait over there." He pointed to another smaller square next to the one we were in. "We need to evaluate the children to see which will be allowed to go to school this year. We will return them to you when we are done. You are not to leave the square while we do these tests," he finished. His accent was strong, but I'd understood most of what he was saying.

I let my mama kiss and hug me and pat down my curls even though some of the other kids looked at me like I was a baby. Then she took my shoulders in her strong hands and shook me hard. Into my ear she whispered, "Behave. Do whatever they say. Be good. I love you."

I tried not to cry when she let me go. She pulled my sister toward me and put my small hand in Anna's bigger one.

"Anna. Hold your brother's hand. Watch out for him. Promise me."

My sister nodded solemnly, then grabbed for my hand. It was sweaty and I wanted to pull away. I almost did but turned to see our mama shake her head. So I gripped my sister's damp hand tighter.

Then we went into the school. I looked at Anna as we walked through the huge wooden doors. It was nothing like she said. There weren't lots of tables and tablets and chalk everywhere. The blackboards were still on the walls, but the rooms were empty of any kind of furniture. As we stood in the hall, they called out names. Boys went one way. Girls another. All too soon Anna broke her promise to Mama and let go of my hand. I was led to a room with Józef and the rest of the boys my age from the neighborhood, and younger ones too. There were even some babies who could barely walk.

"You must help them," a man barked as he followed us in. The door slammed shut behind. He stood and watched. I concentrated on keeping still. The Germans didn't move when they stood, and I didn't want anything to happen if I fidgeted too much. My mama had always said that I was more wiggly than an earthworm. She'd said I got my curly hair because I jiggle so much that the hair didn't know which way to go. I thought that might be true. I also thought it may be because the hair that Papa did have left was curly too. I wasn't sure, though.

"What's gonna happen?" a kid next to me asked.

"Quiet!" the soldier shouted. "There will be no talking."

I turned toward the window and watched the tree leaves move in the breeze. Suddenly, there was a low sound and the stench of the toilet filled the air. I turned back and saw a red stain creep up Józef's cheeks.

I wanted to help him but had no idea what I could do. Mama would have taken me to the bath, filled it with warm water, and wiped me down with a cloth. There weren't any mothers here to do that for him. My eyes met with his for a second. They were dark brown and filled with tears. I didn't want to cry so I looked away, back through the windows at the leaves fluttering light green in the sunlight.

"Who is it?" the soldier asked. "Who has soiled himself?"

No one said a word as the tall black boots walked in between us children. In short order, Józef was lifted by his arms as the soldier held him as far away as his own arms could reach. Once clear of the rest of us, he plopped the boy on the floor. Józef's knees buckled.

The soldier gave him a swift kick, and the boy got to his feet. I didn't think I should watch, but I couldn't look away either. The German man was walking my friend toward the door when it opened. Two more soldiers were bringing in long tables. A third man in a suit was behind them. He looked at Józef and the soldier who had stopped the moment the door opened.

"What is this?"

"Shat himself."

The man in the suit shook his head. "He will not do. Take him to the yard." His blue eyes had pierced us as he said that in Polish. The rest was in German. It didn't sound nice, though.

When I didn't think anyone was looking, I scooted on my butt away from the spot Józef had left on the floor. I didn't know what was going to happen here, but I knew I didn't want to go to the yard.

"Listen carefully," the man in the suit said. "I am Doctor Weber. I need to examine each and every one of you. You will sit quietly until your name is called. You will be very good little boys, do you understand?"

There weren't any girls in the room. No one dared stand up to correct him.

Even though Dr. Weber wasn't looking at me, I nodded. Then I stopped moving my head, because I wasn't supposed to be moving. My mama had said that it was important to be still, like in church on Easter Sunday or when the doctor came to our house. I already knew how to do that.

Another soldier came in. This one had a tall thing that he unfolded. I recognized it as a screen. Mama's friend had one in her apartment separating two parts of the same room. Dr. Weber directed him to move it in front of a table.

"Józef Andrysiak," a soldier called.

No one answered.

The soldier laid his hand firmly on the top of his rifle tilting it toward us.

"Józef Andrysiak!" He was louder this time.

Except for the sound of kids breathing, some coughing and sniffling, the room was quiet. Finally an older boy stood.

"He was here. That was the kid you took away."

I wondered if the soldier had heard him. There was a long pause before he called the next name and the next.

Mama had made up a lot of alphabet games. She'd said that when she married Papa, she'd gone from first to last because our last name started with the last letter of the alphabet.

Every kid had gone behind the screen and then had left the room. Other than Józef, I had no idea where the others had gone. I'd crossed my legs extra tight to keep from peeing on the floor. When the soldier crooked his finger in my direction, I couldn't move.

"You're last. Marek Zamojski. Come here."

I had no feeling in my butt or legs. I tried to stand up but plopped back down almost immediately.

Dr. Weber came from behind his desk and all that much closer to me.

"Is there something wrong with your legs? You looked like the perfect specimen," he said.

"No. They are tingly from sitting here for a long time."

"Let me help you up." He lifted me like the solider had lifted Józef, but his touch didn't seem as rough somehow. "Shake your legs. It will get the circulation going again."

I did as he said and laughed as the tingly feeling jabbed at my muscles. I don't know what happened, but I was grateful I no longer had to pee.

"There you go. Now let's walk to the examination area."

He took my hand. His was cool and dry even after being inside the hot room nearly as long as we all had.

"Take off your clothes."

I looked from him to a nurse standing by. I hadn't seen her before. I wondered had she been in the room the whole time. Her arms were outstretched toward me. I chanced a look between them, then started unbuttoning my shirt as fast as I could. It had always been easier getting clothes off than on.

The rest of my clothes followed. It was much cooler without the fabric. I wiggled my hot toes against the cool floor. It wasn't quite like when Mama let me walk to the edge of a fountain with cold water bubbling through my toes, but it felt good anyway.

When I looked up, a camera flashed. For a long moment I couldn't see anything. When my eyes got better, Dr. Weber was holding up some kind of curved metal instrument. He placed it against my head in several different spots, including against my nose. Lastly, he poked my penis with it. It didn't hurt, but I didn't like it.

"Yes," he said in German to the nurse. Again he said, "yes," then nodded as he wrote in a notebook with a sharp pencil.

To me he said, "You, Marek, give us hope that Poland is not a complete wasteland."

"I like Poland," I said. I didn't know what a wasteland was, but it didn't sound like he liked Poland much. I wanted to ask them if the Germans hated it and us so much, why they'd come. Mama said they had a perfectly good country of their own where they could have stayed.

The nurse thrust my clothes back at me and I put them on as quickly as my mother would have liked this morning. I was even good at the buttons this time. When I looked down, nothing was uneven. I sat on the floor to get my socks and shoes back on. Tying took the longest. One day I knew I'd be as fast as Anna.

Then I stood and waited for them to tell me what to do next. I was getting hungry and wondered what Mama would make for lunch. I was hoping for her egg and goose fat *kanapki* or if there were no eggs, then at least garlic and butter. I knew there was some day-old bread on the counter. Mama had sliced me a piece this morning with my milk. Maybe she'd gone to the market while I was in here and she'd come back with a special treat like *pqczek*. The thought of the pudding-filled cake made my tummy rumble.

"Can I see my mama now?" I asked the grown-ups in the room.

Dr. Weber shook his head and pinned a small piece of paper to my shirt. "Germany is much better. You will see."

5

Whenever the two words "road trip" had come into my mind, I'd imagined myself on some Thelma and Louise type adventure minus the murder and robbery, of course. A conviction was a surefire way to a disbarment hearing before the Ohio Supreme Court. I may not always like my job, but I wasn't quite ready to give it up for good.

On the other hand, driving a rental Fiat from Poland to Germany with my father in the front seat wringing his hands over and over and my best friend in the back, silent and sullen, hadn't been the stuff of fantasies. A crime spree would have for sure livened things up.

I was starting to come to the inevitable conclusion that fantasies never met up with reality anyway. Tom didn't sweep me off my feet. Miles wasn't setting my heart on fire. And I wasn't tossing a bra or my scarf from a convertible on

Route 66, my hair blowing in the breeze. Maybe dreams never came true. Probably why they were called dreams. My life had far too much reality for my tastes, though. A teeny bit of Brad Pitt surely would have turned this mourning mobile on wheels into something fun.

"How long is this again?" Dad's voice brought my wandering mind to a grinding halt.

"Dad." I started to repeat the same thing for the fiftieth, well maybe fifth time, but I was getting a keen understanding of how kids drove their parents nuts. "It's six hundred and twenty kilometers between Warsaw and Dresden. That's—"

"Three hundred and eighty-five miles. Give or take," he calculated.

"Are you some kind of math whiz?" That was Lulu from the back. She'd been quieter than usual all the way across the ocean. I'd kind of counted on her being the buffer between me and my dad's secret past. So far, she hadn't been fulfilling her obligation. Now didn't seem like a great time to point that out, though.

I wanted to blame her out-of-character behavior on Sinclair, though he wasn't here to indict. I still think our former law professor was the wrong guy for her for about a thousand solid reasons. Not the least of which was that he'd changed her in ways that made my best friend lose a lot of what it was to be her.

I leaned a little further toward the windshield, making sure I was in the correct lane. Satisfied I wasn't breaking some Polish vehicle laws, my mind went back to my friend. There was nothing to do at this moment, though. Lulu and Sinclair's relationship was another problem for another day.

My father, on the other hand, was a problem of the first order.

"German education," was my dad's matter-of-fact answer to the math question. Everything that had happened, from the brunch at my parents' house with Lulu as a surprise guest up until this moment, was scrambling my brain. I couldn't decide if my parents had lied to me or I'd been too self-centered as an only child to ask the right questions. I was still settled on the former.

Like a lot of immigrant children, I'd been an easy victim of obfuscation. When many of the answers started and ended with "the old country," we kids had a way of tuning it out. It was a point that Justin McPhee would have appreciated. We'd have laughed about it. Surprised that Justin had penetrated my thoughts, I shook my head clear of him. He was just another on a long list of men who'd disappointed me lately.

Convinced we weren't going to die even without a comprehensive understanding of European driving laws, I took my eyes off the highway for a moment to have a frank look at my father, the man who'd been my closest confidant for all thirty-five years of my life.

"You've never mentioned anything about school in Germany. I'd always thought you grew up in Poland."

"I never said that specifically," he dodged.

"You sound like a lawyer, Dad. That's splitting hairs if ever there was any doubt."

"I am Polish. You've always known that. It's why we're here, no?"

He was clearly being deliberately obtuse. I kind of wanted to give him the kind of look he gave me when he didn't believe the bullshit I was shoveling.

"Dad, I'm driving to Dresden. Which last time I checked a map was in Germany. I'm going to be approaching the border between the two countries in ten minutes by my count. As soon as we cross…" I hesitated. I spoke only German food words and zero Polish ones.

"Lausitzer Neiße." My father read the sign without hesitation.

"What was that again? That big 'b' is an 's'?"

"It's a double 's,' Casey," Lulu said. "It's like the double 's' in the word '*strasse*,' the German word for road or street."

"And since when do you know German?" I tossed over my shoulder as I got close to a bridge. We'd be crossing the Lusatian Neisse according to the teeny tiny English translation at the bottom of the sign below the Polish and German.

"I learned a little in school," Lulu said, surprising the hell out of me. I wanted to pull over right then and toss these strangers out of the car. I wanted my soft-spoken Polish dad and clueless best friend back. Not these people who secretly knew German and hid the details of their lives from me.

"This going to Germany." My father's palm smacked the dashboard. "This was your idea."

"We didn't fly all the way to Poland to sip coffee in cafes and eat pastries," I retorted. Although from the quick peek I'd had into the plate glass *piekarnia* windows, and donuts sold on every street corner, that had the makings of a perfectly good trip. But an internet search into tracing Lebensborn and a long conversation with some Red Cross volunteers was leading us to Germany, of course.

"There's nothing wrong with that. You haven't taken a vacation in ten years."

"No offense, Dad, but Warsaw is not my ideal vacation."

"It was a beautiful city before the war."

"Well, I hope Dresden is beautiful too, because that's where we're going to be in an hour. Tomorrow morning is going to be the first known meeting ever of Lebensborn children. Some of the people there have been searching for their families for months or years. Hopefully, we'll get some tips on the best way to find and approach your mother."

I paused as we crossed the border without fanfare. I imagined it had been very different when my father was born, during the war, and especially after. This borderless Europe was as far from the 1940s as could be.

"I hope she's still alive," I muttered.

I couldn't believe Dad had waited six long months to respond to the call he and my mother had received from Germany. If I heard my mother was looking for me, I'd have moved heaven and earth to be with her as soon as I could. I looked at my father, now an old man.

Of course, intellectually I knew that he'd been a young man once—after all, I'd seen pictures of him at least going back to his teens. But there must have been, if they could have afforded it, another complete set of pictures. Him with his real mother. Her holding him in impossibly white baby clothes that all older pictures seemed to have. Her kissing his fat little cheeks, cradling my tiny father against her bosom. Because all those Eastern European women had big bosoms rarely contained by their stiff cotton clothes in old-time pictures.

"If she is, it's God's will, then. Isn't it?"

"Oh God, Dad. Now the Catholicism?" By the middle of high school, I'd stopped believing in the church. During the height of the sex abuse scandal, I'd even refused to go with my parents for holiday Mass. "How can you still be a believer after what you're now saying happened?"

"Maybe it was God that spared me, Casey. So many others perished in Germany and in the camps in Poland. My own father died during a raid."

"What are you saying?" It took all the effort I could muster to keep my eyes on the road. I was starting to think I didn't know my father at all, and that didn't say anything good about me.

"I don't know. That just came to me. I didn't know I remembered that. I remember the first or second time the German soldiers came through town, they took my father. My mother used to say that he was away working for the war. I don't know if she believed that or was just saying that for our benefit. But my grandmother told me the truth. She said he'd been shot for being a threat to Germany."

I tried to focus my mind on the map I'd studied in the morning while it reeled with this new information. None of which I'd ever heard an inkling of before.

"It was called Intelligenzaktion," Lulu started. "Before the invasion, the Germans made a list. The rich, influential, nobility, professors, doctors. A list of one hundred thousand who they systematically killed so there was no one to lead the opposition to the occupation."

"You say that like you're reading from a textbook. Are you serious? I've never heard of this."

"Jews weren't the first or last target of the Nazis. They wanted to roll through Europe, and for the most part they did. What they had going for them was a systematic plan of execution, pun intended."

"Jesus. How did I not learn this in school." I had to turn my attention back to the road as we were closing in on Dresden.

Not travelling had done me a disservice. Though I hadn't heard of Lebensborn or Intelligenzaktion six months ago, I remember being lectured about the bombing of Dresden during World War II. Intellectually, I knew not to expect bombed-out buildings and Germans in tattered coats with hollow eyes. But somehow that's what I thought I would see.

The bucolic little city with its classical architecture and picture-perfect bridge did not jibe with the war-torn city in my mind.

"This is…pretty. What river is this?" I asked as I crossed a bridge and navigated along cobblestone streets toward our chain hotel. The last time I'd stayed at a hotel had been during the bar exam.

Same chain.

It had been another city—Columbus—on another river—Scioto, but these two cities couldn't have been farther apart if one was on Earth and the other Mars.

In my mind, East Germany had been turned into one gray concrete Communist mecca. To see that it looked not much different than it probably had in its pre-Soviet days set my expectations on their ear. Nothing was what it had seemed only a couple of weeks ago.

"Elbe," Lulu answered.

"Should have paid more attention in geography," I muttered as I followed the signs to the tiny parking lot.

Thirty minutes later we were checked in. We were sharing something called a junior suite. Lulu and I would share a large bed and my dad would take the pull-out couch in another room.

I plopped my suitcase on one of those wood and strap numbers and popped the locks.

Lulu was lying on the couch looking out at some grand building that had to be an ancient church.

"How old do you think that is?"

"A thousand years."

"It survived the war?"

"Nope. It had to be rebuilt stone by stone after the collapse of the Berlin Wall."

"I'm thinking you missed your calling. How do you know all this stuff?"

"I don't know anything really. My grandparents traveled all around Germany. My grandmother's father, my great-grandfather, I guess, was some kind of cantor. He went around singing and praying and whatever else they do, taking his family with him. My grandmother and all her brothers and sisters moved from synagogue to synagogue until they left Germany in the mid-thirties and came to Akron."

"So *your* family history was an open book?" I couldn't help the small dig at my father.

"For the most part. Maybe it's part of the 'never forget' legacy, though. I mean, my great-grandparents bought their way out by selling everything they had. Their brothers and sisters and cousins, though, stayed because they thought it could never get that bad. Because they wanted to keep their flats, and money, and positions. None of them came out. I would say no one talks much about that because it seems, maybe, that there were some lucky ones and the rest weren't pessimistic enough."

I pulled out pants and long-sleeved button-down Oxford shirts and put them on hangers hoping to keep the wrinkles down. I added my low-heeled flats to the wardrobe, then slipped the stack of papers I'd received by fax the day before we'd boarded the flight to Warsaw.

At the desk in the corner, I spread out the pages and slid my finger along the faded words until I found it.

"Dad. The meeting is tomorrow. It's at something called Kreuzkirche is the way it's named here. I think that means the Church of the Holy Cross. There's a meeting room. You're to be there at two in the afternoon. What do you want to do in the morning?"

My father turned from the window he'd been peering out of and looked at me like a deer in the headlights. He took a long moment to compose himself before he spoke. I was waiting for him to correct my pronunciation, but he didn't.

Instead he said, "I'm going to read through these documents the Red Cross sent. To see if I can make heads or tails of it all. You and Lulu should spend the morning touring Germany. It's not the country it was when your mother and I left it."

They'd been in Germany? Together? I wasn't even sure if I'd known that. I wasn't sure of anything anymore.

6

"I, uh, need to step out for a moment," I said to Casey and her dad before hightailing it from the hotel room. It was hard to keep up my double life while we were all in close quarters.

I hadn't traveled with my own family in years and kind of forgot how on a trip like this everyone is practically in each other's pocket. I hadn't talked to Sinclair in a couple of days, but as soon as I turned on my phone and connected it to the local network in Germany, there were no less than ten messages on my voice mail. In every single one of them, he was insistent that I contact him immediately.

I took my time pressing the down button on the elevator, exiting and walking through the hotel lobby, then following the street through a tunnel toward the river. At a stoplight, I navigated the busy traffic across the cobblestones until I was in a crowd of people taking a ferry from Dresden to some German town I'd never heard of.

I wanted to call him back, or maybe I wanted to *want* to call him back, but every time I lifted the phone ready to dial the long string of international digits, my fingers froze on the little gray buttons.

"Hast du ein ticket?" a man in a white shirt, epaulets gleaming in the sun, asked me.

I slipped the phone into my pants pocket and looked up at him.

"No...nein. Es tut mir leid." I'm sorry. No.

He gave me a genuine smile, a mini-salute and walked to the ferry, jumping aboard and hooking a chain across the space. Another man untied what was probably a sailor's knot and threw the rope toward the boat. A horn hooted and the boat chugged away up the river.

Practically alone now that most of the crowd was gone from the riverside, I found a bench, pulled the phone out and dialed.

"It's two in the morning."

Embarrassment made my hand shake. How had I forgotten something so basic as the time difference?

"I'm sorry, I can call you back later when you're up."

"I'm awake now. Give me a moment."

I heard fumbling with the phone as it hit something hard. I watched more boats move up and down the river. I took the time to look at all the old buildings, some of which had to have been reconstructed. I wondered why I couldn't have fallen for some guy my own age. Maybe if I'd left Cleveland instead of playing it safe, I'd have had the guts to put myself out there instead of living in a city where everyone judged me by who I had been in high school and law school. I gripped the phone harder when I heard Sinclair's voice again.

"How is Poland?"

"I'm in Germany right now."

"But you flew to Warsaw."

"The search for Peter Cort's mom has taken a short detour in Germany. I told you that I would probably travel between a few countries. They're all in the EU now, so it doesn't make much difference."

"I just feel more comfortable knowing where you are."

"What's going on? You left messages." It was my effort to turn the conversation from me forgetting to check in. Trying to talk to him about something I couldn't fix almost always led to an argument. With jetlag nagging at me, I wasn't up for it now.

"Deborah and I have talked, and we've agreed to get a divorce," he said. His voice was different this time. He'd promised this before, but I could tell he was dead serious now.

Elation and dread filled me in equal parts. At that exact moment, I wished I'd paid more attention to Casey's discussion of her law practice. I had no idea what to ask about the process or how long it would take. Or whether it meant that he and I were to marry at the end of it. I'd hated that he was married, but it kept the issue of the culmination or advancement of our own relationship at arm's length—where I'd liked it.

"What happened?"

"I told her that I didn't love her anymore. That we shouldn't stay together out of obligation."

"Okay."

"I was hoping you could put me in touch with Casey. I'd appreciate her advice, if not her representation."

Of all the things I'd worked through in my mind, that wasn't one I'd seen coming. I'd never been the smart one in my family. That was David. Becca had been runner-up in brains and the winner in beauty. Until I'd started dating Sinclair all I'd had going for me was quirky. I looked down at my gray slacks and ice-blue sweater. Now I didn't even have that.

"She's not back until I am."

"I'll wait. I want someone who's familiar with Ohio family law and sympathetic to my cause."

"Sympathetic?" Cause? That one I didn't ask out loud.

"No one likes to see a guy leaving his older wife, no matter how beautiful and accomplished, for a younger woman. But since that younger woman is her best friend, I think it could be a great relationship. Plus it's full of irony."

"Irony?" It was all I could say. I didn't want to touch that beautiful-and-accomplished part with a ten-foot pole, because I knew that I was neither.

"I represented her before the law school's judicial board during that brouhaha. Now she can represent me."

I sat on a bench and did the slow blink. His representation of Casey had been...well...unenthusiastic. She'd lost her position and a lot more. Hopefully she'd do a better job, if she took the case, of course.

"So you'll talk to Casey?" he asked. I knew if I didn't at least agree to something, he'd never let it go.

"When I get a chance, Sinclair. This trip is pretty serious, and I want to give her some space."

"Okay. No worries. Maybe during a lull in the trip. Just bring it up a couple of times in casual conversation. Then, she'll be prepped when you all come back. That's not too much to ask my soon-to-be fiancée."

"Fiancée?" I was embarrassed by the breathless sound of my voice.

"If your best friend's any good, I could be single this time next year. Think about where you want to get married. I can't wait for you to come home. Remember to call me in the morning, okay? My time. Check the zones before you call. It's a nine-hour difference."

"I'm not sure of the schedule yet. Her dad may have a meet—"

"Just a quick check-in. If you call me at seven my time, I should be up by then. Can't wait to talk to you when I've had a full night's sleep. Look, I have to get back to bed to make sure I get my full eight. I'm shit without it. You know that. Love you. Talk to Casey. Good night."

Then there was nothing but static. I pulled the phone back and looked at the screen, indicating fourteen minutes and twelve seconds had elapsed during the call.

"Lulu! I thought I might find you by the water."

I stuffed my BlackBerry in my pocket before she could see it in my hand.

"Casey? I'm looking at the Elbe. Pretty riverfront they have here."

"Dad's ready to go to eat. The hotel recommended a casual bierhaus around the corner. He's already on his way over. I figured I'd find you and we could walk together. Did I interrupt something? Looked like you were on the phone."

"Just checking my messages. Making sure there's no one at work that needs me."

"At close to three in the morning?"

"Well, if there's anything, I could address it when they wake up before we go to bed."

"You're making me nervous. I haven't called Cleveland since we landed."

"Who's taking over your practice?"

"Letty will call if any emergencies come up, but I continued my hearings so it should be pretty quiet over the next couple of weeks."

"Are you taking divorce referrals? After the Hudson stuff, I wasn't sure what you'd ultimately decided."

"What's the case? I won't turn down money. And since you're making the referral, there will definitely be money, right? Was that one of the messages from your office?"

"It's Sinclair."

"Sinclair?"

"He's asked his wife to divorce him. He asked me to marry him. I think we're both engaged."

7

Marek

July 15, 1942

"Hast du schon wieder in dein bett gepinkelt?" The nurse was fully in white from her head to her toes. She was in charge of everything. But I didn't understand a single word she said. There were two other children, one boy and one girl who spoke Polish. But we only whispered in the middle of the night when the nurses and matrons went away.

I shook my head. I repeated the first German phrase I'd learned, *"Ich verstehe nicht."* I don't understand.

A lot more rapid German came back at me. Then Nurse Schröder grabbed my wrist and pulled me back to the big room all of us kids slept in. The walls were white. The floors were nearly as white and made of cold tile that felt good under my toes during the hot mornings of the last few weeks.

My cot was in the far corner, near a window. It was cold some nights by that window. But when wind whistled through cracks in the wood, no one could hear me cry.

She put my hand down in the middle of the thin mattress I'd slept on for the last three or four nights. I'd already lost count. My cot was cold and wet. She pushed my head down and yelled more words.

I wanted to tell her I was sorry. I wanted to tell her that I'd never done anything like it at home. Instead I lost control…again. This time, I could feel the warm trickle of pee running down my leg. Nurse Schröder turned away in disgust. I stood there for a long time not knowing what I should do. What I knew I shouldn't do was to go upstairs to breakfast where all of the other children were. My stomach growled, but still I didn't move. I nearly peed myself again when I heard shoes squeaking on the floor. I turned around and breathed out in relief. It was the nice nurse.

"Let me take you to the bathroom," Nurse Nowak said in Polish. She spoke both languages. She put her hand out and I grabbed it. It was warm like Mama's. I hiccupped as I tried not to cry. Nurses hit the boys for crying. Never the girls. It was one of lots of things that weren't fair. Like the fact that I couldn't see Mama or Papa.

"I can't stop it," I explained while Nurse Nowak stripped off all my clothes and threw them into a bin. The bathroom was also white and spotless. Sinks lined one wall. There were bathtubs and showers on the other side. Toilets with dividers between them against another. The last wall was all windows which were open. I shivered at the thought of being cold even when the breeze was warm.

Nurse Nowak wet a cloth. I waited for the shock of cold water, the pull of goose bumps. Instead it was warm. So warm after days of cold baths.

"Are we going home soon?" I hadn't dared to ask the question of anyone since we got here. The kids who asked too many questions got the strap. One kid who couldn't stop crying was carried out by two men dressed in white. He never came back. Nights got very quiet after that.

"You're going to have to learn German. Otherwise you will not be able to stay here."

"Does that mean I can go home?" The Germans had clean rooms and more food than I remembered having at home, but I'd rather be hungry with Mama and Papa than full in this strange place.

"No...not home. Someplace worse where there is not enough food or any heat. Like a prison for children. Learn German. You're young enough and smart enough to do it."

"I don't like German," I whispered so as not to have my voice bounce around the tiled room. "It sounds like everyone is mad all the time."

Nurse Nowak's light blue eyes looked toward the door for a split second, then came back to me. She stared at me hard. She didn't blink. She put the cloth under running water, soaped and rinsed it twice before coming back to me. She washed me again as gently as she could with the scratchy cloth. Then she squeezed out all the water and hung it on a hook. I waited while she stepped outside and came back with a towel. She dried my whole body, then pulled me back toward the sleeping room. My cot was stripped bare, the gray fabric on the mattress stood out in a room where every other was covered with white sheets.

"I will help you. It will be our secret. If you learn German, you will go to a good family. A rich family who will give you only the best."

For a moment I imagined having my own bedroom, my own shiny new bicycle, lots of fresh bread and sausages and cheese in a big brick house where we didn't share a court yard. Then the image faded as I realized Nurse Nowak didn't say anything about me going to this rich place with my mama and papa and even the grandmother I didn't really like.

"What about Mama and my sister? Can they come too?"

"Unfortunately, there is a war going on. You can not go home right now, and they can't come to be with you."

"Do you know where they are? Are they in Germany near here? Can they come and see me?"

"Travel is dangerous. Europe is full of men shooting at each other and bombs being dropped. It's too dangerous to go back. This is the only place that you're safe right now. Learn German and you will be safer. Do you understand?"

I didn't understand. Not quite, but I nodded anyway because a prison for kids sounded awful. No food. No heat. Probably no hot water, ever. It was summer now, but I knew it would get cold again. Mama had always been very careful about coats and mittens and scarves and all of that.

"Now, you are to go upstairs and sit for breakfast. Ask Nurse Schröder for a bowl of porridge. Repeat after me. *Kann ich frühstücken?*"

I stumbled through the pronunciation three times before I could get the words, *can I have breakfast*, right.

"Always say thank you when anyone here does anything for you. Say, '*Danke.*'"

"*Danke,*" I said. "Thank you" hadn't been that hard. It was a word that kept the nurses from frowning or swatting at our legs.

"Listen to everything they say in lessons. Memorize it all. When we are alone, I will teach you more." She grabbed my shoulders and shook me violently. I had to swallow hard not to start crying again.

"To stay alive, you must learn this. I tell you the truth when I say that the Nazis will starve you to death if you do not get this right. You look perfect. Your blond curls. Your blue eyes. Get rid of your Polish and it will save your life."

She'd shaken me as hard as Nurse Schröder did, but I knew that Nurse Nowak did not mean it in a bad way. It was the way that my mother had grabbed me before I'd left her in Poland. It was filled with love and fear in equal parts. That kind of feeling had always scared me. It was no different now. I nodded and promised in my best Polish to do whatever she said. Just like I'd promised Mama.

8

If I had a bucket list, and if it included travel, I can't imagine that I'd have added an austere room in a cold stone-walled church to my list of must-see destinations.

I counted twenty people in the room, not including me. All of them were gray-haired and well over sixty. Of course, they'd have to be because the war had ended some sixty-one years ago. Trying to look like I wasn't looking, I scanned the room while the elderly folks helped themselves to pastries, cakes, and cups of coffee and glasses of water. I'd made it a point to resist eating even though the smell made my mouth water. The aroma of baked goods was a dead ringer for the smells that came out of my mother's kitchen.

"Why haven't we ever visited Germany?" I asked my father as soon as he sat down with his own coffee and cake in hand.

"Do you know what the Germans call the time of mass murder during the war?"

"World War II?"

"'Our dark past.' Ask. Listen. I know that Dresden looks pretty on the outside, but this country has a festering wound on the inside."

I blinked several times at his strong words, then sat back in my chair, extending my legs. I'd worn brown corduroys with a white turtleneck and even then I was the most underdressed person in the room. The men wore blazers and sport coats. Many of the women—dresses. I'd heard Paris was formal, but this...

A tall man with thinning hair cleared his throat and stood. Then he spoke in German, which for some reason I hadn't expected. I turned to my dad for an explanation. He scooted his chair close to mine and gave me the highlights.

The man speaking had done extensive research on the program and his own origins. He had been the one to reach out to the people in this room as well as the Red Cross. He asked everyone to go around the circle and introduce themselves. Soon enough it was my father's turn. He spoke first in English. That was probably for my benefit.

"My name is..." He faltered right after that first sentence. There were nods of understanding from most of the people in the room. After a long hesitation, my father continued. "My names are Peter von Kraus, Marek Zamojski, and Pietrek Cort. My...my Polish mother, my birth mother or her family is searching for me. I was like all of you, taken from my original family and placed with a German one, the von Krauses. I emigrated to Cleveland from what was then East Germany in nineteen fifty-eight after I married my wife, Birgit. This is my daughter, Casey. She's an attorney in Cleveland."

While he repeated the whole thing in German that sounded perfect in its pronunciation, I appraised my father. He had three names? Only one of which I'd ever heard. He had an entire life, an origin story I knew nothing about. I could tell you that Peter Parker was from Queens, lived with his aunt and uncle when he was bitten by that radioactive spider, then made his own superhero suit complete with web shooters. But I couldn't have given as detailed a history about my own father.

Shame and embarrassment filled me. When another person spoke English, I tamped down my own feelings and tried to pay attention. I was here to support my father, not beat myself up for being shut out of his earlier life.

"My biggest flaw is that I have an excellent memory. I have a vivid recollection of being in a school classroom and having my whole body measured while the doctors and nurses whispered that I didn't have any Jewish qualities so I could be Germanized. First I was shipped to Bad Polzin. Then Kohren-Sahlis. They had adoption parades. Eventually, I was adopted by the Schreck family. They were close to the Führer."

"Have you found your first family?"

"No. That's why I'm here. I've hit a dead end at the ITS in Bad Arolsen."

"I may be able to help you." This was from a small, thin, pale man I hadn't noticed in the hour or so we'd all been in the room.

Nods came from nearly half the group.

"Some call me the 'Father Finder,'" he said. "I'm good at research."

There were murmurs of protest and some talking in German.

"I may have more success than others. I can help you and Ms. Cort. Let's meet after and we'll discuss it. I don't want to derail this meeting."

I spent the remainder of the meeting watching the "Father Finder." I was intrigued by a guy who could speak at least two languages and had access to some kind of central research. I'd heard the same thing everyone who'd studied history had—that Germans had kept meticulous records during the war. I was relying on this trait to be the key to finding my grandmother and other family in the couple of weeks I'd allotted for the trip.

Even though it was probably rudely American, I immediately went to the Father Finder the minute the meeting concluded.

"I'm Casey Cort. Peter is my dad. Maybe you can help us?"

"Jürgen Friedrich." He offered his hand, and I shook it. "There's a little room we can talk. Please follow me."

I waved at Dad, then beckoned him to follow me to where the Father Finder was directing us.

"How did you come to us?" Jürgen asked Dad, once we were seated in the room.

"A call from the Red Cross. They say my mother is trying to find me but couldn't really provide much more information. The address and information she left are no longer good."

"How long ago did she start her search?"

"I think five or six months. Maybe a lot longer. I'm not sure," Dad said.

"Mm-hmm. How long are you in Germany?"

Dad looked at me. For a man who'd been in command my entire life, he looked a bit...lost. I picked up where he left off.

"We're staying at the Hilton, though our tickets were in and out of Warsaw. We figured she'd likely be in Poland. We drove here because maybe the records are in Germany, but she was in Poland. What do you think?"

"Did you rent a car?"

"Yes." I nodded.

"Let's drive to Bad Arolsen in the morning. It's a four-hour drive. The ITS is in the process of opening up its archives to the public."

"Isn't this the Nazi research center that has been closed, for what? Sixty years?"

"Not closed exactly. Only victims, next of kin, and Red Cross employees had access."

"So most of the 'people' with 'access' were those who'd perished?"

"It was started to reunite those displaced by the war. It expanded to include those persecuted when it started archiving the extensive records the Nazis kept."

"So that record-keeping was true? Seems like this should be easy, then."

"There's a caveat."

"Isn't there always."

"While there are a lot of Lebensborn documents in the archive, many of the records were destroyed."

"Why those?"

"When the liberating armies came through, orders came down from on high to destroy all the records in this program. Wasn't the same for others, but very specific for this one. So what was there was set on fire. Probably came down from Heinrich Himmler himself. He was the founder of the program."

I'd heard of Himmler of course. Of Hitler as well. But to think that a high-ranking Nazi official had a direct effect on my very existence was chilling. I was used to being one born in the land of the free and home of the brave. Knowing that was really a fluke of fate was somehow unsettling.

"So what are the chances? Is a trip to this Bad Arolsen a good idea?"

"Bad means spa," my father interjected. "Probably a pretty town otherwise. Germany is full of lovely areas. You and Lulu may enjoy it."

Friedrich looked between us...assessing for a long moment. "Since your mother came to the Red Cross, there's a good chance of cross-referencing that with what your father has and coming up with a result."

"So, Dad, are you game?" I asked giving the two of them my own assessing look.

"I guess." His shrug was ambivalent. "Since we came all this way..."

9

When I'd put my BlackBerry in my jacket pocket, I hadn't anticipated another person in the backseat with me. When the so-called "Father Finder" turned his head toward the window, I slipped it out of my pocket and looked at the screen.

Richard Sinclair: It's 6:29 in the morning here in Cleveland. That means it's already 12:29 in the afternoon where you are. Why haven't you called?

If being a lawyer had taught me anything, it was the ability to master rapid thumb typing on this tiny device. I surveyed my surroundings. Casey had her eyes glued to the road worried as she was about German drivers even though she'd studiously plotted the trip to avoid the autobahn. Peter—though now I knew that was about four steps removed from his real name—was looking out the window.

The glass reflected back such sadness that I had to blink and look away. Jürgen Friedrich...I repeated the name five times to myself to commit it to memory...his reflection was one of a man at peace. I kind of wondered how he did it. Maybe it was being European or something. I can't remember looking at an American face that wasn't full of anxiety. Sure that no one was watching me, I turned back to my BlackBerry.

Me: Driving from one city to another. It's at least three and a half hours more.

That last was a lie, but I needed a buffer between now and our next check-in.

Richard: Are you driving? Using your Blackberry while driving is dangerous.

Me: Casey's driving.

Richard: So there's no reason you can't call me now. I need to know that you're okay.

Me: I'm not comfortable calling you. There's a stranger in the car.

Richard: Who?

Me: Jürgen Friedrich. I dare you to say that three times fast.

Richard: There's a man in the car with you? Who is he?

Me: He's a researcher. We're taking him to the ITS with us.

Richard: Send me a picture.

Me: I am not taking a picture of this guy. That's weird.

Richard: No weirder than you being in a car with a strange man. How old is he?

Me: I don't know. At least fifty. Maybe sixty? He's old. Not my type.

Richard: A little bird told me that you have a thing for older guys.

Me: I have to go. I'll call you later.

Richard: You better.

"Boyfriend?" Friedrich's voice came out of the blue and scared the crap out of me. He was smiling at me in the indulgent old person way that said they were thinking and reminiscing more about the past than talking to you, the real-live person sitting before them. In fact, I was willing to bet the next words out of his mouth would be something along the lines of "when I was your age" or "I once knew this girl…"

"Lulu, you promised. We had a pact." Casey interrupted, never giving Friedrich that chance to stroll down memory lane.

"A pact?" Casey's father turned from the window and looked between us.

"We *agreed* to take a man break. For the time we're here, I wasn't going to talk to Miles and *she* wasn't going to talk to Sinclair."

"Sinclair?"

"Daddy, do you remember the professor who botched my honor code disciplinary hearing. The same professor who let someone else's bad deed become mine? Well, he's the one Lulu is seeing."

"Well, what does it say about your so-called engagement that you want a break from Miles? Shouldn't you be over the moon and not be able to take a single step away from him?"

"We're independent adult women with careers who don't need men in our lives." My best friend's voice was a little strident. From the backseat, I couldn't give her the kind of nudge I wanted to. The kind Sinclair gave me when I said too much.

"Maybe you don't *need* someone, Casey. But some of us might *want* someone," I said.

"We're not fifteen, Lulu. I don't think it's a good idea to live in each other's pockets."

"I like his pockets," I said. He was the first man who cared enough about me to actually ask what I was doing and whom I was with. With other guys I'd dated, it was out of sight, out of mind.

"His pockets seem to require constant attention. Why do you have to check in with him one thousand times a day? Why aren't you wearing your old clothes?"

"For...fu...for goodness' sake, Casey, did you expect me to dress like some bohemian forever? If I want to make partner, I need to dress the part. That means blouses and skirts and—God save us all from self-destructive clothing—stockings. Even heels."

"You can barely walk in heels."

"I'm learning."

"Do you want to work for a place that requires you to change your entire personality to cash a check twice a month?"

"I certainly don't want to have to hang out a shingle and work for myself."

"Touché."

"Oh, Casey, don't take it personally. You're on a hard road. I don't want to be on a hard road. I've been slaving away at Dalton Lacey for a freaking decade already, and what do I have to show for it?"

"A fat salary? An office with a window? The ability to work on pro bono cases and still keep the aforementioned fat salary?"

"You're not wrong. But I want the recognition of being a partner. Some kind of job security. The ability to control the kinds of cases I get. The challenge of running them."

"And blouses and skirts are going to get you that?"

"My rhinestone glasses and Technicolor coat haven't." Dalton Lacey was supposedly one of the most progressive firms in the county, but maybe Sinclair was right. He was in on partner meetings after all. Maybe my over-the-top behavior was holding me back from progressing up the career ladder.

"Fine. If that's the reason, I'm fine with it. If it's to please Sinclair, I'm so not fine with it."

"What difference does it make *why* I'm doing it? Why shouldn't I want to please the man I'm with?"

"I did that tie-myself-in-a-pretzel thing and you know what? It didn't work. Sinclair should love you just the way you are. I do."

"It's not like he bosses me around. He's a partner. He made some suggestions on how I could join him up there in the rarified air of his forty-fourth-floor corner office. I took them. End of story."

"That by no means is the end of the story." Casey looked at her father, probably realizing that we weren't in the car alone. We couldn't talk like best friends talk. "I still think we should keep to our pact."

"How do you suggest I convey this to Sinclair? I'd love to talk, but my best friend and I pinky-swore that I couldn't."

"Tell him you're busy. We are…busy. I think we've only got about thirty minutes left anyway. Partnership stuff aside, there are still very legitimate reasons I don't think Sinclair is right for you."

"Those reasons have changed, Casey. I think we should talk about this later."

"You're not talking to Miles?" Casey's father put to her.

"Dad. It's a girl thing, you wouldn't understand."

"Aren't you going to marry him?"

"Yes, of course. Maybe. No. I don't know. It's not an easy thing to decide."

"Not easy? I met your mother. I loved her. We got married. I'm still happy I made that decision."

"You're not calling her every five minutes."

"I've spoken with her."

"A *normal* amount of times." Casey practically threw that into my lap in the backseat. "Anyway. Miles wants to get married right away."

"I'm sure the church could accommodate you."

"He wants to elope, Daddy. His parents are getting a divorce, and he doesn't think they can handle a wedding right now."

"Divorce is a grave sin. Could they not work it out after all those years together?"

"After thirty-plus years or whatever, I'm sure that they're past the working-it-out stage. Plus they're not Catholic, so maybe they don't enter the sin category. I need time. I told him. So that's that. I'll make a decision when I get back."

Friedrich cleared his throat from his backseat bird's eye view to all our dysfunction. "You'll need to turn off in about eight hundred meters."

Casey hit the turn signal.

"That's a half mile," I translated. "Can we not do the old lady blinker thing."

"It's less now. I'm not turning it off."

I turned to the Father Finder. "So when we get there, what's the plan?"

"The plan is to find Herr Cort's mother. I see no reason we shouldn't be able to get it done before the end of the day."

10

The train ride from Kohren-Sahlis to Meissen was slow. We kept starting and stopping. Soldiers got on. Soldiers got off. Different soldiers roamed the aisles checking everyone's papers. Except for us. One of the matrons from the home was traveling with us. She answered all questions and the soldiers passed us by without document inspection.

"You two are quite fortunate," the matron said to me and the girl who'd been assigned to sit next to me. "Viktor von Kraus has agreed to take you in. He's a very well-respected officer. His family has been pivotal in providing the Reich with weapons that will help defeat our enemies."

I looked at the girl next to me. Like I was to be called Peter, she was to be called Anna, just like my real sister at home in Poland. When the matron left us alone, I immediately leaned toward the girl.

"Are you Polish?" I whispered in Polish.

"Shhh. You'll get us in trouble," she responded in German.

"Where are we going?" This time my whisper was in German.

"My family was killed during a bombing, so they're adopting us into new families. We should be grateful. Otherwise we'd be orphans in a war. Nurse Nowak told me they are all starving because of the war."

"Do you think my family is dead?" This was in Polish again. I was swallowing heavily to make sure I didn't cry. Germans didn't much seem to like crying.

"Probably. Why else would we be here?"

I turned toward the window squeezing myself as close as possible to the cool glass. In my heart, I knew that Papa was probably dead. When Józef's cat had died, he'd called me over to see it. It didn't move, even when his dad lifted it and put it in a box. If Papa were dead, did that mean he didn't move? But Mama...I couldn't imagine her not moving. She was always moving. Cooking. Cleaning. Hugging me. I had to close my eyes hard so that I didn't think of her dead.

"Promise me, Agata." I used her other name.

"What?"

"Promise me that we can talk in Polish in secret. When no one is looking. Okay? I'll need to be able to talk to Mama when I go back home."

"If I promise you, will you only talk in German all other times?"

I nodded.

Hours later, at a train station that looked no different than the many others we'd passed, matron said, "It's time." She yanked us both out of our seats, and before I knew what was happening, Anna and I and our bags were on the platform. Wistfully I watched the train chug away to the next town, leaving nothing but steam behind.

"Where are we?" Anna asked.

Matron smiled. "Meissen. You two are the luckiest of the children we've placed this year. Herr von Kraus has agreed to do his duty for the Reich and take you and Anna as his children." Matron looked at her watch. She summoned a porter and he lifted our bags. We followed the adults through the big square building outside. A large black car pulled in front of us, and a chauffeur came around to open the back door. A man and woman stepped out. The woman looked like she was from a movie poster. The man had on a fancy army uniform.

Matron dropped a stack of papers not once, but twice after Herr von Kraus offered to help retrieve them.

"I am Ilse von Kraus and I will be your new mother." The fancy woman took the papers from Herr von Kraus. "Let's see. You are Anna, and you are eleven years old."

Anna curtsied like she'd been taught in the home.

Frau von Kraus turned to me. "And you are Peter. It says you're six."

I didn't bow or anything, but I did keep my eyes down. I nodded. "Yes, ma'am."

"They look a little thin," Frau von Kraus said to Matron or Herr von Kraus, I wasn't sure.

"Yes, well. These are war times. We're doing the best we can to save the Aryan children. They've had meat at least twice a week, and fruit every day. I'm sure that with the right diet, they'll become robust and thrive in your home."

"Yes. I'll have Cook prepare hearty meals for them starting with supper." To Anna and me, she said, "Are you ready? Come along, then." At our hesitation, she looked us up and down. "Have you never been in a car before?"

I shook my head hard. Anna took a step back when the engine roared to life.

"There will be a lot of first times, I suspect," she said, pushing me and Anna toward the backseat. We each squeezed in, taking our place between our new adoptive parents.

"Be good children," Matron said before turning quickly on her heel and walking back into the big ugly bahnhof.

After a few minutes, the car pulled up a long drive. Frau von Kraus led us in through a side door until we were standing in a very warm hall where I could hear the sounds of pots banging and pans slamming.

"I am very sorry that your parents have died. But we're at war. The sacrifice of our citizens will be honored when the thousand-year Reich flourishes. We are your parents now." She pushed us into a kitchen where a long wooden table sat heavy with bowls of chopped vegetables and a raw chicken.

"Cook will make you dinner. After you eat, she will show you to your rooms. Herr von Kraus and I must go out this evening. Senior officers are in the city and we must see them. Until tomorrow."

She left us at the table. I took a seat on the bench. There was one woman in the room cutting something. The room smelled like fresh baking bread. I hadn't smelled that smell in a long time. Not since the last time Mama had taken me to get the bread first thing in the morning. We used to go every day. After the war it wasn't as often. I didn't know I'd missed that smell.

"*Chleb*—" I turned around when I felt a sharp pain on the back of my neck.

"No more Polish."

"I'm sorry. I didn't—"

"I've heard the nurses talking. The Germans have killed a lot of Polish people. They will kill us if they think we're anything other than German. Do you want to die?"

"What are you two whispering about other there?" Another woman had come into the room, but I hadn't heard her. Agata...Anna pinched me, on my arm—hard.

"I am Peter," I said in my best German.

This woman had eyes that were kind. I hadn't seen eyes like those in a long time. She stuck out her hand. I took it and tried to shake it like I'd seen men do.

"I am Greta Heinrich. I'm the bad sister."

"Bad sister?" I repeated.

"I...how old are you?"

"Six."

"Never mind. Who is this behind you?"

"A...anna."

"You're here too. How nice. Just between you and me, my sister, Ilse, is no fun. Her husband even less fun. Now, you two look like kids who can have a good time." Greta surveyed the food preparation. "Dinner's not for an hour at least. Come outside with me. I want to show you something."

She was dressed in the oddest clothes. Like the kind that the workmen had worn when they were fixing windows or leaks around the home. There were three or four different colors of paint on them. Her hair was coming out of a messy knot. It was like she crackled with energy.

To keep up with her, Anna and I had to run pretty fast. After a few minutes, we came upon a huge lake. I had to stop so suddenly before I slipped down the damp grass and fell in. She led us on a long walk around the entire lake pointing out animal tracks and good places to hide.

"Isn't this great?" Greta said when we were almost back where we'd started. "Look up."

Anna and I obeyed. Above us was a rope dangling from a fat tree limb.

"What is it?"

"Rope swing. You climb up. Someone gives a push, and you can swing over the water. If it's warm enough, you let go and drop in with a great splash. It's amazing fun even if you don't let go."

"Can we try it now?" I asked.

"Maybe tomorrow. If we don't get back and eat dinner, cook will tell on us and my sister and her husband will be very mad. We don't want that. Plus, it smelled good back there. I think there's going to be a roast chicken."

My mouth watered and any thoughts about swinging and swimming were abandoned in favor of focusing on my stomach, which growled loudly.

"You *are* hungry. I should have saved this. Let's go eat. I'm so glad that you're here. Finally some fun around here."

11

"This is very...institutional." Both Friedrich and Lulu looked at me as if I'd farted in a closed elevator. "What? This place is kind of weirdly impersonal and depressing. Animal rescue is warmer, and they kill pets there. Would it be too hard to have some photos on the wall of families embracing, reuniting, that kind of thing?"

"You mean propaganda?" Friedrich said. I hadn't met that many people since we'd landed, but the comment felt very East German post-communist to me. Suspicious of anything that evoked positive emotion.

"We call that marketing in the US," I said.

"I suppose you would." He looked at his watch. "Frau Pohl should join us shortly."

We followed his lead and took seats in the waiting area. Dad and Friedrich sat in adjoining chairs, Lulu and I opposite them, also side by side. I took a look around and wondered if this had been the origin of the word austere.

Even though she'd tucked her phone deep, I could still hear the beep. Not once. Not twice. The third time, I jabbed at her with my elbow.

"C'mon. What's up with Sinclair?"

"How do you know it's him?"

"No offense, but I don't think Dalton Lacey thinks you're quite that indispensable."

"I have a huge favor to ask you."

"Sure. You came on this fishing expedition with me." For which I was indeed eternally grateful. This would have been a lot if I'd been on my own with my dad. "I'm happy to return the favor. What's up?"

"It's a big one."

"Okay."

"No, really big."

"Please spit it out. My mind already has you pregnant with Sinclair's baby, him having dumped you, and you asking me to be your birth coach and move in with you to help you get through those first few months of infancy. Then my cat, Simba, gets mad at the interruption in her twenty-three-and-a-half-hour sleep routine, and jumps out of my bedroom window in protest but survives to live another day because—cats."

"Wow. I kind of wish you'd had brothers and sisters around when you were a kid. You would not have had this kind of time to spin stories in your head."

"So?" I prompted.

"Sinclair is leaving his wife—"

"We talked about this in Dresden. Does that mean you guys will 'officially' be together? Does that mean you'll get married? Are you pregnant? Is that what you want to discuss?"

"I am *not* pregnant," Lulu hissed, sneaking a glance at my dad and Friedrich. Deep in conversation, neither was paying much attention to us. "Sinclair wants to know if you'll handle his divorce."

If she'd slapped me I couldn't have been more shocked.

"I kind of thought you were kidding before. There are tens of thousands of lawyers in Ohio."

"You'll be discreet. Nonjudgmental."

"That's what he told you. He thinks I'll be nonjudgmental. So let me get this straight. When I asked him to represent me, he did a half-assed job and basically fucked me over. Am I supposed to return the favor? 'Cause I think that may be malpractice."

"How many times do I have to apologize for that?"

"Zero times. You were not the wrongdoer. Dean Condit, the other editors on law review, the Strohmeyer family, even me for being naïve, but not you. Never you. You were one of the only people to support me for all these years."

"Will you—"

"Herr Friedrich, Herr von Kraus?" The rest of what the primly dressed woman said was in German, but I got the gist of it from watching my dad stand and make to follow her. Lulu jabbed me and we brought up the rear. She led us to a small room with a wood table and six metal chairs around it. On the ink-stained surface sat a thin stack of documents.

"What's this?" I asked Friedrich.

"What they have concerning your father's adoption."

After offering us water, not to be imbibed near any documents of course, Frau Pohl stepped out leaving the door ajar.

I picked up a document, scanning for some kind of clue. If my handwriting had been as neat and precise as it was on the papers, I'd have saved myself all sorts of grief in Catholic school penmanship lessons. I put the documents back down and pushed them toward the men who'd gravitated to the other side of the table. Friedrich quickly scanned them and then pushed each, one at a time, toward my father.

Dad's breath was barely audible as I watched him look through the thin stack one page at a time. I stood and walked to the other side of the table once curiosity got the better of me.

"What are you seeing?"

He smoothed a sheet, then pointed his finger at a faint line of writing. "Peter" was written along with some German, then Herr Viktor von Kraus with an 1896 date.

"Peter," he read, "is to be adopted by Viktor von Kraus and his wife, Ilse von Kraus, whose maiden name is Heinrich."

"What are all these others?" I poked a finger at a long list of German names.

"It's the names of their families going back several generations."

"It's a mini family tree," Friedrich interjected. "To make sure that the Aryan child is going to a pure family with no Jews in the lineage."

My eyes snapped to Lulu's. The eyes of my best friend didn't look mad or angry, just kind of resigned.

"Don't mind me. I get it. It's why what's left of my family is in Cleveland and not here," Lulu said.

"So where's info on your family? Your...original family from Poland." I eyed the thin stack.

Dad riffled through some pages, then extracted one that was a crude photocopy of only part of a half-destroyed piece of paper. I followed his finger. He was pointing to a name, "Marek Zamojski," and another name: Zamość.

"How is that even pronounced?" Accent marks over consonants was a new one. Differed from what I knew of Spanish or French or even German.

"It's my hometown. Where I was born."

"You always told me that you came from Dębniki. Was that just a lie?"

Dad pulled the first paper out and laid it on top. "You see this date?"

"Fourteen, or is that seventeen, nine, nineteen forty-four."

"That was when the von Kraus family took us in. Right before the war ended. I was six. I knew I was from Poland, but somewhere along the way, I lost the name. Greta told me much later, after the von Krauses had defected, that Anna and I were from Dębniki. I didn't have any reason to disbelieve her."

"Do you speak Polish?"

"Not really."

I took two steps back. I wanted to think that he and my mother hadn't deliberately lied to me, but I was having a hard time wrapping my head around this new information.

"Where did you get the name Pietrek Cort?"

"When I came to America, I didn't have a complete set of papers. I didn't want to say I was only German because it wasn't true. So I used the Polish form of Peter."

"And Cort." I'd taken so much pride in that name. The first Cort to go to college. The first Cort to finish law school. The obvious irony of having a last name that sounded like "court," while practicing as a litigator.

It was like the idea of myself and my family were built on a false foundation that was crumbling down around me as I sat in this generic block of a building.

"It sometimes means 'brave' in German. Your mother thought leaving was brave of us."

Like in some awful movie montage, I spun through the memories in my brain like papers flying out a window or calendar pages flipping.

"Mama went along with this?"

Dad nodded. "We wanted a fresh start from the horrors of the war."

I stopped talking and leaned against the wall behind me. The cool plaster was rough beneath my hands. I hoped it didn't snag my sweater but didn't care enough to lift myself away from the surface.

"Aren't we here because your mom was looking for you?" Lulu asked.

Dad nodded.

"So where are those documents? These seem important and all, but you can take copies of these to go. What about something from your mother?"

Dad and Friedrich paged through the thin pile. They both shook their heads.

Lulu stood. "Frau..." She looked back.

"Pohl," Dad filled in.

"I wonder if she's Polish," Lulu mused in low tones before calling out, "Frau Pohl! We need some help in here."

"What if she doesn't speak English," I protested.

"I'm betting she does," Lulu said as the woman came to stand in the doorway.

"Did his mom come here looking for him?"

"Yes."

"So where are those papers? I mean, this historical stuff is interesting, but that's not the reason we flew all the way to Europe. All this we could have gotten by fax."

"Fax?" Frau Pohl wrinkled her nose in misunderstanding.

"That doesn't matter. How can we get the information his mother left here for him?"

"This is not a relay service."

"But your original mission was reuniting families postwar, right?"

"Yes. Of course."

"My friend's dad, Peter von Kraus or whatever, wants to find his...birth mother from Poland."

"The von Krauses were a very important and influential family in Germany. They owned a porcelain factory," Frau Pohl intoned.

"While I love a good history lesson as much as the next person," Lulu said, "now's not a good time. I'm from a Jewish family that fled, so you can understand that a nostalgic journey through Germany's past isn't my thing. How do we get the documents?"

"Let me talk to my colleague," Frau Pohl said before retreating back through the door.

"Lulu!" I reprimanded sharply. That was the best friend I'd known and loved, but I hadn't expected her to get her groove back at precisely the wrong time.

"What? All the smiling and making nice may work if you're playing the long game like our man Friedrich here. But I don't have time for that. We have tickets back. Your dad ain't going to live forever, no offense. And if his mother is still alive, she's got an even shorter window—"

Frau Pohl came back in the room with a man who was impossibly paler and gloomier than she was.

"I think this may be what you're looking for," he said. He handed over a single index card to my father.

He took it and read it silently. Nodded. The ITS staff stepped back out.

I pushed myself from my wall perch. "What does it say?"

He placed it on the table. I looked over his shoulder again. This time the date was more current as was the handwriting. It was from February of this year. It had a name Erika Zamojski and an address in Krakow. Attached to it was a photocopy of a picture of a young boy, maybe four.

"Is that you?"

Dad traced the picture. "I hated that shirt. It was scratchy, but Józef's father had a new camera. Promised to take pictures of all of us. I remember when he'd come back with them. Mama pinned them all up on the wall. Me. Papa. Anna." He didn't say anything more. I didn't think he would be able to for a while. Which was fine as we had a long drive back to Poland.

"Now what?" I looked at Frederich, then at Lulu even though the question was rhetorical. Even though the next step was obvious. "Now what?"

12

"Are you going to ask Ronja to the party? It's the last one this year."

I swallowed down the peach pit-sized lump in my throat. Ronja was the most beautiful girl in the school. With long dark hair and dark eyes, she stood out from all the other fair-haired girls. Every boy in every year had a crush on her. I was just one among many.

"She's turned every single boy down."

"Do you think any of them really asked her? She will say yes to you."

"Why me?"

"You're a von Kraus. Everyone knows your family."

"It's just a family like any other," I protested, though I knew it wasn't like any other. I'd stayed at the house in Meissen with Anna and the von Kraus family for only two years. It was chaos after the war was over, but we were never hungry, and the Soviet soldiers never bothered us. Which was much different from my school mates whose families did not own the town's biggest employer.

Then they'd sent me here to Bad Kösen Country School which most Germans couldn't afford. I'd felt like they were sending me away because they'd regretted the adoption during the height of Third Reich nationalist furor. Even though that may have been the case, I was happy for it. The school was warm and welcoming. Maybe because of the war, there were more girls than boys. It made for a great variety of people to think about at night as I was falling asleep in my room.

"Really."

"The school motto talks about everyone being equal no matter the background," I said, in case anyone was listening. "That's what the new German Democratic Republic has in all the posters we see."

"Either way, you are one of the best-looking boys here."

I wished that were true, but my hair was curly like a girl's and flew all over the place in the wind. I wasn't as tall as a lot of the boys either.

"This is the last one?"

"The housemaster says it has to be. We go home for the Pentecost, then we have our final exams, then we go home for the summer. She doesn't want us thinking about parties in June when we should be focusing on studying."

"Fine, I'll ask her."

"When?"

I wasn't sure I believed in God but maybe fate, because Ronja stepped out of the front door right at that moment and started walking by where we were sitting on the stone portico.

"Hi, Peter," she said with a smile.

The curve of her lips somehow dissolved the stone in my throat, and I was able to speak.

"Ronja, we were just talking about the party this weekend. Would you like to go with me?"

"Peter von Kraus, I thought you'd never ask. Of course I'd love to go with you. I have to go talk to my history teacher. I don't think I'm doing that well."

"Dinner, then," I said. I was proud that my voice didn't crack.

Despite the chill in the air, I was warm all over. I even smiled when the housemaster approached me.

"Herr von Kraus," he said, handing me a slip of paper. "This came from the office. They want to see you by the end of the day."

"I'll go now," I said. I didn't want anything to get between me and dinner with Ronja. I left my friend and the housemaster under the stone arch of our dormitory and took the five-minute walk to the building that housed the administrative offices of the school. I hadn't been in it more than a handful of times.

"Herr von Kraus, how can we help you?" the receptionist said.

"I got this paper. It says something about the bursar?" I knew he handled money, but I didn't know more than that. Herr von Kraus, the man I now called Father, handled the money. He paid for boarding fees and books and gave me a few deutsche marks for treats. I didn't have much money left now that the end of the year was near. I made a mental note to call and ask for more, so I could buy Ronja flowers or candy before the party.

"Yes, of course. Please go down the hall there. It's the third door on the left."

I followed her instructions. A woman with wire-rimmed spectacles and hair almost as curly as mine sat behind a desk with a large adding machine in the middle. She was punching at the numbers, and white tape was spilling out the other end when I stepped in.

"Herr von Kraus." She stopped her calculations. "Please close the door." I did as she requested. Then, at her gesture, took a seat on the hard wooden one facing her. "You are the last student I expected to see in here. Unfortunately, I have to talk to you about fees."

"Fees?" I echoed.

"Your boarding fees have not been paid for the last few months. We've tried to contact Herr von Kraus and then even Frau von Kraus, but our letters have come back unanswered."

"Have you called?" I asked. Our family had been one of the first in Meissen to have a phone installed.

"Your...aunt? Greta Heinrich has not been much help. That's why we're talking to you. Unfortunately, the state will not subsidize housing. We need you to go home and talk to your family as soon as possible so that we can resolve this." She handed me a train ticket. "Your housemaster has bought this for you for tomorrow morning."

"The last party of the year is tomorrow night," I said in protest.

"Surely you understand that this is more important than a party. There will be many more of those in the coming years."

I took the ticket in hand. "Fine, I'll go talk to Father." I sighed in resignation, my dreams of kissing and touching Ronja in all her soft places going up like smoke.

I tried to put Ronja out of my mind during the ninety-minute train ride back to Meissen. I'd had to tell her at dinner that I had a family emergency. I even brandished the ticket the school had bought for me to lend credibility to my story. Her look of disappointment filled me with regret that I hadn't had the courage to talk to her in the last year and a half. I spent most of the train ride kicking myself over being so timid. When I stepped out of the still ugly station, I promised myself if I ever got the opportunity again, I'd go for it right away. What was the point in waiting? If the war hadn't taught people anything, it should have taught us all that.

I looked right and left hoping to spot Father's car and driver, but the curve of pavement in front of the station was empty. After waiting for a futile half hour, I lifted my small suitcase and walked to the bus stop, immediately regretting not taking the first two buses that had come and gone in the meanwhile. I stepped aboard the third about a minute before a downpour started. I hadn't thought to bring an umbrella, so I was a damp mess when I made the kilometer walk from the stop to the main house.

I had to knock a long time before Aunt Greta answered.

"Peter. You're a mess. Come in. Come in."

The house was as quiet as a cemetery. The usual smell of bread and sausage was noticeably absent as were a few pieces of von Kraus heirloom furniture.

"Where's Cook?" I asked as my stomach growled. I'd skipped the offer of a meat sandwich on the train, saving room for the hearty sausage, potato, and kraut dinner I knew would be waiting.

"I had to let her go."

"Why?" I said, fearing the worst. The Soviet soldiers had been unkind during their occupation of our part of Germany. For many nights I'd feared the worst would happen to Mother or Greta or Cook, or even worse, to my sister,

Anna. But after the war, Father still had enough money and influence to keep them safe.

"The state has expropriated the porcelain factory."

"The state took it over?" Greta nodded, sadness etched into her features. "Oh. I didn't know."

"Viktor thought he'd be able to work out something, but the government was unrelenting, even with a factory of historical importance."

"Now what?"

"He and Ilse have moved to West Germany. They're going to start a new factory there. He somehow put aside enough money to get across and buy a business there. Jews owned it, I think, and it went up for auction."

"Moved? What about this house?"

"They've left me in charge. I'm a painter, Peter. Most of my patrons have left. I have just enough money for a little food and coal in the winter."

I shifted on my feet wondering how the reason for my visit was going to go over.

"I...my school sent me here to get money for boarding fees. Father stopped paying five months ago. Should I call him at his new house?"

Greta's face looked so pained I was afraid to ask more. To speak more. Because in my heart I knew what was coming. I said it for her.

"There's no more money for me, is there?"

Greta went to the secretary in the corner, the one piece of real furniture that remained. She extracted a slim envelope.

"Viktor asked me to give you this. You're to call the man whose name is in here. He's agreed to take you on as an apprentice."

I took out two slips of paper and read over the first. It was the name of a machinist in Lipcse and an address. The second sheet was a letter of introduction. I searched my brain. I didn't even know what a machinist did.

"He worked with Viktor in some capacity before and during the war. I'm not sure about the details of that." Greta waved a dismissive hand. She'd never concerned herself with the details of anything. I'd loved that about her when I was a kid, but I wasn't sure it would serve her well in this new communist future East Germany was building.

"What about school?"

"I'm sorry, but there's no more money for that. Nor university after. He's done you this favor though, so all is not lost. Why don't you go up to your room? I'll put together some bread and cheese and beer for supper."

"What about Anna?" I asked of my sister. We'd traded a few letters, but I'd mostly relied on Greta to keep us apprised of what was going on in each other's lives.

"He got her a place with Ilse's seamstress and his haberdasher. They're a lovely couple with no children. I think they lost their boys to the war. They're willing to train her, and she can take over the shop when they retire."

I didn't want to cry. Especially not in front of Greta. So I took her suggestion and went upstairs. There would be no more school. No more Ronja. Once again, life as I knew it had changed as quickly as the weather had today. Like the clouds buffeted by the wind, I had no choice but to go along.

13

"Dad, they all look the same, just pick one and let's go," Casey shouted at the bathroom door.

"You gotta cut him some kind of slack. He doesn't know what he's walking into," I said to my impatient best friend.

"And it's going to matter if he's wearing a plaid shirt or a plain one?" Casey tapped her foot. Fortunately, the carpet muted her.

"It's not about the shirt."

"He's going to make us late," Casey said. Her foot increased its rhythm. "Dad! Come on. Friedrich is in the lobby. We're supposed to be there at one and it's five after twelve."

After a couple of odd-sounding thumps, and the tap turning on and off, Casey's father emerged from the bathroom. The button-down shirt was blue, tucked into dark gray slacks. The shoes were shiny black leather and matched the belt. Based on my sartorial history, I didn't offer advice, but the outfit seemed perfectly reasonable for ninety percent of anything he'd encounter.

I looked down at my own yellow turtleneck and brown slacks and suddenly wondered if it was too much. Following Sinclair's lead, the sparkles, rhinestones, and boho-chic were banished to the back of my closet. I was still working on taking his other suggestions of keeping the colors muted to heart. White, black, beige, and gray seemed boring enough to make me fall asleep in front of the full-length mirror.

Bending to tug at the zipper of the faux snakeskin boots I hadn't yet relegated to the donation box, I decided what Sinclair didn't know wouldn't hurt him.

I read the room and decided that maybe now wasn't the time to pester Casey about representing Sinclair. But my BlackBerry was buzzing in my pocket with what was probably his tenth message in two days. I wasn't at all clear why it was so damned important that Casey represent him. I mean, it's not that I didn't think she probably wasn't a total kick-ass lawyer or something. But he wasn't a professor anymore. With his Dalton Lacey big firm salary, he could afford the best of the best in Cleveland. But after being with him for more than a few months, I knew once he had a bug up his ass about something, he wouldn't let it go. Which was why I was picking up a plain wool coat from the desk chair where I'd dropped it and not my favorite patchwork quilt one that was hidden at the very far back of the closet in my childhood bedroom. I'd rescued it from the giveaway pile he'd made in the middle of my living room floor in the spring.

I took the lead and led our little procession of three down the hotel stairs. It was an early twentieth-century building like many of the others around us but had been rehabbed completely on the inside. Despite that, I still wasn't one hundred percent on board with the tiny little elevators Europeans stuck in any nook they could find.

"Good, you're all here." Friedrich stood. "Let's go. Casey, you're driving? Or do you want to take the tram. Either way, it'll be about half an hour."

Casey jingled the rental car keys. "Let's drive."

I knew she'd want a place for her father to be alone after whatever was happening. There wasn't any way it wasn't going to be emotional.

Friedrich sat shotgun with a city map in his hand. In quiet tones, he directed us from our boutique hotel in touristy Old Town to a neighborhood called Podgórze across the narrow river that bisected the city. My parents had taken us kids to Europe several times when we were teens. We'd toured concentration camps, remaining synagogues, Holocaust memorials, and some famous secular buildings.

My memories of European vacations were bogged down with houses of terror and actual displays of fabric reams of yellow stars in all the various languages. I knew that this neighborhood we were driving to had been a Jewish ghetto. I'd probably been here after a tour of the Kazimierz. If memory served, we were going to be near the original Schindler factory. My family had, rightly so, spent a lot of time talking about the Jewish casualties of the war. But sitting next to Casey's father, I was seeing firsthand how much more widespread the atrocities were. Sometimes that war seemed like the gift that kept on giving.

The BlackBerry buzzed again, and I glanced around the car. No one was paying a lick of attention to me. The two in the front were navigating both the language and the streets. Casey's father was looking out the car window deep in thought. I fingered the device and a message popped up on screen.

Sinclair: No call today. You okay?

Lulu: Not a good time. We're about to drive to Casey's grandmother's house.

Sinclair: Will she take my case?

Lulu: You sound like a desperate client.

Sinclair: I am.

Lulu: I don't know. I'm going to turn this off now. We can talk later.

Sinclair: At least tell me that you're dressed appropriately. No bright colors or anything like that.

I looked down at my mustard yellow turtleneck and thanked goodness phones hadn't developed into Jetson's-style videophones. When the car was parked parallel to a curb, I held down the button to power it off and shoved it deep into the pocket of my appropriate coat.

We all exited the car. We all stood silently for a long moment on the sidewalk. It wasn't even my family and I dreaded finding out what was on the other end of this quest. Friedrich folded the map in his hand into a very small square. Shoved it into his breast pocket.

"It's just around the corner."

We all walked down the block, then took a right until we came upon a pre-war indistinctive building. Friedrich removed another piece of paper from his pants pocket and compared the information to the directory affixed to an electronic box on the panel beside the door. He pushed a button next to the number thirty-five, and electronic ringing came through the tinny metal speaker.

"*Cześć?*" I had to assume it was some form of greeting.

"I have Marek Zamojski with me," he said in English.

Without any other words, the buzzer sounded. We all looked at each other before Friedrich pushed the heavy ten-foot-tall wooden door open. It led only to a large hall with mailboxes, utility boxes, and more steps. As we trudged up the stone, I shivered. The air inside was colder than outside.

On the second floor, we pushed open a door that led down a balcony. A woman opened one of the apartment doors and stepped out. She'd probably been a mousey brown-haired woman at one time, but the few dark hairs she had left were nearly overtaken by gray. I pegged her age somewhere in her late sixties or early seventies. Not old enough to be anyone's mother.

As our little entourage advanced, her hand went to her mouth as she let out a gasp.

"Marek?

It was as if all the years had melted away from Casey's father's face. I could almost see the scared little boy he'd been all those years ago when Poland had ceased to be his home.

"Anna? Is that…" He stuttered through the same question in German, then in the Polish I'd heard all around me while we'd been in Warsaw and Krakow.

The older woman nodded, then she reached out her arms and he stepped into her hug. The two of them stayed like that for a long time.

"Can you speak Polish anymore?" she asked in English when Peter pulled back a few inches. He extracted a handkerchief from somewhere and wiped at his now damp eyes.

Anna did the same with the sleeve of her loose cotton sweater.

Peter shook his head.

"Erika!" she shouted.

A woman came to the door. I figured she was probably little more than a decade older than me and Casey.

Somewhat formally, she shook Peter's hand, then the rest of ours.

"I'm Erika, Anna's daughter. I can speak English," she said with a fairly heavy accent, though I had no problem understanding her. "Please come in."

Casey accepted the invite by stepping in first. I followed, with Peter and Friedrich bringing up the rear. We each took a chair around a round wood table. The apartment was bordering on stifling, so I put my jacket on the back of the chair. Remembering her manners, Anna held out her hand for our coats and disappeared with the thick pile for a minute or two. When she came back, she was carrying a tray with a coffee or tea urn, cups, and a platter of pastries and cakes. I stood and helped her get everything to the table without incident.

"How long have you been in Poland?" Erika asked.

"We landed a week and a half ago. We drove straight to Germany to get information from the various organizations," Casey answered.

For a few minutes, the only sounds in the room were those of cups and spoons and plates and forks as Anna made sure everyone had coffee and a treat. For nothing better to do, I took a bite of the cake I'd been served. It was, I had to admit, a little slice of heaven. I'm not sure what I thought would greet me here in Poland, but charming pastries had not been on the list.

I wondered, for the first time, if I'd been as much of a victim of propaganda as we'd been taught that those behind the Iron Curtain had been. Almost everything about Poland had been a surprise. From the large swath of historical buildings not destroyed by war to the sunny weather outside.

Every picture I'd ever seen of Poland had been filled with gray people in gray clothes under even grayer weather standing in a long line for something: food, democracy, or maybe absolution for being on the wrong side of history.

For a moment, I forgot everything that Sinclair had impressed upon me about waiting and thinking before I spoke.

"Where is your grandmother?" I asked Erika. "The call…Casey's dad got in April said that his mother was looking for him."

Erika's face went white. Anna poked at her. It was a long moment before Erika turned to her with a translation.

Fresh tears sprung from Anna's eyes. Erika stood and retrieved several tissues from a box on a sideboard.

For the first time, I think I understood why Sinclair was always chastising me. I spoke first and only realized later, often far too much later to fix it, that I'd talked out of turn. This appeared to be one of those moments.

Erika turned to Casey and her father. "She died on Easter Sunday."

"They only called on Good Friday," Peter said in protest. "Two days before…"

"We'd put in a request to find you last year," Erika said. "When *Babcia* Maria first got sick."

"How did she…what did she…"

"She had a bad heart. It failed." Anna poked at her daughter again. Spoke with a sense of urgency. "Mama says that her heart was broken beyond mending when you were taken away by the Germans."

"What happened to you. After I left…?"

Erika finished the coffee in her cup. Sighed. In her heavy accent, skipping over words that she couldn't quite remember in English, she translated for Anna.

They'd gone home after the gym assembly. Mama had asked for information, but no one would say anything. Eventually, a German officer visited our house and told Mama if she didn't want anything to happen to *Ojciec*—our father—then she should stop asking questions. We only learned later that Father had been long gone by then. He'd been killed right outside of town during the German raid when he was taken away.

Mama tried again after the war, but information got harder and harder to get after the Soviets took over. Once the so-called Iron Curtain fell, it was impossible to learn more.

"Last year when she…" Erika said, speaking for herself again. "When Grandma got sick, Mama and I went to the authorities to look for you one last time. I called the tracing service in Germany. This time they said they might have information and would contact you. That was right around Christmas."

Everyone at the table was quiet again. There would be no such reunion or happy ending like this in my own family. When we'd been in Germany more than a dozen years ago, the only traces of my own heritage were a list of names of those who'd perished in the camps etched on a synagogue's memory wall.

Erika and Anna turned to Peter…Marek and he gave a broad sketch of his own life. School in Germany, apprenticeship, coming to America. Working, retiring. His life at St. Ignatius parish.

"My daughter, Casey, is a lawyer in America," he said proudly. I laid a hand on my best friend's back at this proclamation. I could feel her tense up with the mixture of pride and expectation in his voice.

"I am a nurse here in Krakow. Mama used to work in hospitals helping out patients and I...you would say followed in her footsteps, right?"

At our collective nods, Erika smiled.

"I'm engaged to be married," Casey blurted out. I couldn't help the sharp turn of my head. She must have been more certain than I'd thought. "My fiancé, his name is Miles. He gave me this ring," she said, extending her hand onto the table.

"That's very...beautiful," Erika proclaimed.

"It's non-traditional. He didn't want to do the same thing everyone else did."

"Have the two families gotten together for the engagement party?" Erika asked.

"Not yet. Miles' parents are in the midst of a divorce, so it's—"

"Yes, I could see how that would be awkward," Erika interjected.

"I...let me..." Anna stood and disappeared. In a moment she was back with an aged album.

"These are pictures of Grandma." Erika proffered the thickly bound book. Peter took the album carefully, laying it between him and Casey. I scooted my chair over so Anna and Erika could stand behind them. For a long time, Peter flipped one page, then paused to examine the small black-and-white photos, his fingers lingering over the faces.

"Do you remember this?" Erika translated. Anna was smiling. Bouncing on her feet. I looked over to see that it was a full family shot. Candid. Each of the kids had a lollipop or some kind of sweet in their blurry hands.

Peter was quiet for a long moment. Too long for polite conversation. I wanted to jump in and say something, but Sinclair's admonitions swarmed into my head. I clamped my lips shut. Casey looked expectantly at her father.

He stood up abruptly. Erika and Anna stepped back in surprise. He turned toward the window near a couch on the far side of the room, then strode over. He cast his eyes about like he was taking in the traffic. If I were a betting woman, I'd have said he wasn't really seeing what he was looking at.

"I'm sorry. I can't do this. I am not your Marek." He looked at Friedrich. "I'm not Peter von Kraus either. I'm Pietrek Cort."

"Daddy, of course," Casey soothed as she stood and joined him. "You get to keep your name."

"It's not about a name, Casey. It's that I don't remember Marek. I don't remember that little boy in any of those pictures. I don't remember anything about Poland. I don't remember you, Anna. Worst of all, I don't remember Mother either. I thought coming here, looking at pictures…some of this would jog my memory, but none of it does. I'm sorry. I'm not the little boy you're looking for. He's long gone. The Germans took him away in nineteen forty-two."

14

October

"There's a girl out front. Can you see what she needs?"

I put down my tools and wiped away the grease from my hands with a rag. Finally, after years of watching and waiting at Herr Schiller's shop, I was going to get to handle my first order from start to finish. As East Germany grew separate from West, our business was growing. Finding replacement parts for many things was difficult if not impossible. I'd learned a lot about how to fabricate almost anything anyone needed. But it was lonely work. The opportunity to talk with someone other than the dour-faced Herr Schiller and his wife was welcome.

I pushed my way through the leather curtain that divided the back from front.

"Can I help you?" I asked. The woman had her back to me, examining a brass fitting that was sitting on a shelf, fiddling with a paper tag with the customer's name who was supposed to pick it up.

She turned around and smiled at me. Her smile was dazzling. All thoughts of Ronja and regret, thoughts I'd been carrying around for two years disappeared just like that.

"I am Birgit."

"Peter. Peter von Kraus. How can I help you?"

From a handkerchief, Birgit let a deformed piece of metal fall onto the counter with a metallic thud.

"My father, he is a baker on the other side of town. This"—she pointed to the part—"makes the steam in the oven. It has stopped working." She leaned closer, her voice a whisper. "The German ovens are far superior. We do not want to replace it with a Soviet-made counterpart." Her voice returned to normal. "If you could make another, that would be helpful."

I picked up the part. It was a nozzle. One that probably released water or steam at certain cooking intervals.

"I can make another, no problem. This time it would be brass. A little more expensive, but more durable than steel."

"I'm so happy to hear this. A new oven was not in our budget."

The light from the windows filtered through Birgit's hair, making it look like a soft pale halo surrounding her face. Her pale blue eyes caught mine and I nearly lost my breath.

"It would go a lot faster if I could come look at the oven. Get some information. Take some measurements."

This was not entirely true. I could, without leaving the shop, replicate this broken piece with near-perfect accuracy. But I didn't want her to disappear, to never be seen again. I didn't want to take that chance.

"It would be best if you come now," she said like I'd hoped. "The last batch should be out of the oven by the time we arrive. It will be off for the remainder of the day."

"Give me a moment to get my coat," I said. I ran in the back only coming to a stop when I came up against Herr Schiller's smile. It was rare to see anything but a frown upon his face.

"She is beautiful, no?"

I could only swallow and nod.

"Take her home. Look at her oven. Stay for dinner if they invite you. It is not natural for a man to be alone too long. The four years you've been here are too long. She's a beautiful girl. Go make friends."

He didn't have to tell me twice. I shrugged on my leather jacket wishing it didn't have a grease stain on the right cuff. I put that hand behind my back and walked out to the shop front.

"Shall we take the bus?"

"Yes, my stop is just across the way. After six stops I have to change to another. You're sure this is okay?"

"It's important that we get these things right," I said.

When we boarded the bus, it was mercifully empty as the grandmothers had already done their shopping and were back at home cooking. It was in between work shifts. School had not yet let out. I was grateful for the quiet.

"Where are you from?" she asked.

"Meissen. I am Peter von Kraus, by the way."

"Does your family own the porcelain factory?"

"No, not the famous one. A far more utilitarian one. Although Father has moved it to West Germany."

"You didn't go?"

"My aunt Greta is still here. Our family house also. It's my responsibility to stay. It will all be better when Germany reunites."

"I am saving up to go to America," she whispered. "After what's happened in Budapest last year, I'm not sure about the future of Europe. A cousin visited from Cleveland. She says that it's a land of opportunity. There are no shortages. There are no lines. If I work hard there, I can have a comfortable life."

"You are very pretty," I said. Dumb. So dumb. "I am surely not the first man to tell you this."

Her smile was coy. "It's nice coming from you. You are quite handsome yourself. I like your hair. Is it Kraus because everyone has curly hair?"

I lifted my hat, brushed back the curls that had escaped, then pulled the wool back down to keep the hair in place.

"A coincidence really. I'm the only one."

"A throwback, then?"

I followed Herr Schiller's advice. Took measurements. Accepted the dinner invitation and the one Birgit extended for a post-dinner walk along her quiet street.

On the lonely and long bus ride home, I was again grateful that the vehicle was nearly empty. I stared out of the window reliving everything from the moment Birgit had walked into the shop until I'd kissed her on the cheek some eight hours later. From the time I'd moved in with the von Kraus family until this morning, I'd never been sure of much. Life seemed like it was carrying me along like a toy boat on the river current. For the first time, I felt like I could change direction, that I could determine my own future.

I wasn't sure of anything else, but I was sure of one thing. I would marry Birgit Vogt.

November

"There is a new passport law coming in December. If we're going to leave, we have to do it now."

I knew that Birgit was right. Things had only become more restrictive over time. Reports of increased checkpoints and patrols had filtered from Berlin to our part of Germany. It was why we were on the train to Meissen. I hadn't been home in a good long time. Without the von Krauses, and without Anna and Cook, it was bleak somehow.

"I don't have a passport," I said.

"Let's do it all now, get the papers squared away. If your father vouches for you, says he needs you at the new factory, that should be enough," Birgit's voice was a whisper, but her sense of urgency came through nonetheless.

"There's something I need to tell you," I said. I had fallen in love with this beautiful girl. I'd proposed to her, planned to spend the rest of my life with her. I was the luckiest man in the world. I took a deep breath because when she found out I wasn't who she thought I was, maybe she wouldn't think she was so lucky.

"What is it? Do you not want to get married? Is it too fast?"

"No. That's not it at all." I moved closer to her. Put my hand over hers to quell any unfounded fears. "It's nothing to do with that. I'm adopted."

"Adopted?"

"During the war, there were homes for the orphaned children of German soldiers."

"I'm so sorry. When did you come to Meissen?"

"Nineteen forty-four. I was six."

"Do you remember your parents?"

"Only that my father must have been stationed in Poland, because I know some Polish words. A few."

Unlike the von Kraus family, Birgit didn't seem to put a great deal of store in my supposed lineage. She reassured me during the remainder of the train ride that who my parents were didn't matter. Her eyes didn't even get big on the walk up the drive to the large manor house. I knew then, in my bones, that I'd made the right decision.

"Greta, this is Birgit." I introduced them the moment my aunt opened the door.

"How lovely you are, dear," Greta said, patting the place where Birgit's hair escaped her hat and met her shoulder. "I'm Peter's aunt. My sister and her husband left me to take care of this pile of bricks."

"It's a beautiful house," Birgit said. She craned her neck to get a better view.

"It was," Greta said. We all stepped inside the vestibule. It wasn't quite chilly, but it wasn't warm either. "I can't keep it up much anymore. I've closed off most of the rooms so I'm not using so much coal. I paint, sleep, and take my meals downstairs now."

"Birgit and I want to get married." That came without any preamble. It was like growing up during a war had eliminated the need for all the niceties.

"Congratulations!" She hugged each of us for a long time. "This is such good news. The best news I've heard in a long time."

"I need my birth certificate," I said. "The registry office has a long list of required documents, but that's the most important." Birgit and I had inquired once we'd decided that marriage was what we'd wanted.

"All the important papers were kept in the drawer of Viktor's desk, but he took that. He did leave some boxes in his study, though. Why don't you have a look through those.

I'll put on the kettle for some tea. There's also a bit of cake left over from a bit of a splurge I had over the weekend."

"You never eat cake," I said. Greta lived on paint fumes and air. She loved sausage but hated pastry. It was a fact that Anna and I had loved because it meant more for us.

"I'm seeing one of the Soviet officers," Greta said quietly.

I could feel my face pull into a deep frown. For most of us, the Russian soldiers had been and continued to be our enemy. They wanted to make East Germany into a prison and us into inmates.

"He's different," she insisted.

"Is he around today?" I asked. Birgit's widened eyes met mine. We'd have to be very circumspect if there was a soldier around. They were all de facto spies.

"No, he's off to a meeting in Dresden. He'll be back at the weekend."

"Birgit, why don't you come help me with these," I said in a bid for privacy. "Give me about half an hour, then we'll come down and have cake with you." My aunt disappeared into a back room after she waved us away.

The boxes were in the corner exactly where Greta said they'd be. I lifted one lid, only to find nothing but business documents. A second were related to the house. A third bank statements.

"This is probably it. You should have a look," Birgit said from the other side of the room where she'd opened her third box.

I went over and looked inside. There were some pictures of Anna and me. Greta too. In a thick folder were what looked like identity documents. I sat on the cool floor and pulled out a sheaf of papers. Those that related to Anna, I put aside. Her little kid face looked so stern, her blond hair as straight down as her lips were across.

Then I found my picture stapled to the top corner of a few pages. It acknowledged my adoption. Then I looked at the document underneath. It was in small handwriting. Another picture of a smaller boy. I peered closely. Was it me? He was so little and so thin. If it hadn't been for the curls lifting from his head, I'd have had my doubts.

From the script, I could only tease out a name: Marek Zamojski, and a location: Zamosc. I looked at the spelling, then back and forth between all of the lines. The last word took some time for me to read, the writing was barely legible. That word was: Polen. I was so confused.

"Peter? What's wrong?"

"Nothing. Please give me a moment. I must talk to Greta alone. It's family business."

I took the stairs two at a time, my feet echoing on the wood. I wondered why the rug that used to cover the stairs was gone. The brass holders oddly had remained in place.

"Aunt Greta!"

She was in the kitchen standing by the sink. The cake was sitting on the table, a striped towel that had probably been covering it was lying next to it. The tea server, polished to a high sheen, stood at the ready.

"What is it, Peter? Were you unable to find the documents?"

I thrust the incriminating pages at her. "What is this? Who is this Marek and why does it say he's from Poland?" I wanted to pretend that it was a mystery. Deep down in my bones, though, I knew. Flashes of memory that I'd always associated with dreams collected in my mind.

"Am I the son of a German officer, killed in battle?"

"No...no. You were an orphan. Many children were orphaned. Our government saw it as a duty to take in those children who could...adjust...be integrated the best."

"That's it? Why didn't anyone tell me this before."

"We thought you knew. When you and Anna first moved here, you'd speak that language with each other when you thought no one was listening. Eventually it stopped."

"So I'm Polish?"

"You're German. As German as I am."

"Then, why can't I get identity papers?" My first couple of tries at various government offices had met with resistance, even when I made the war an excuse. "I need them to marry Birgit. To get a passport. We want to travel to Albania for a honeymoon." The last was a lie, but no one announced plans for defection. That was enough to get one sent to a reeducation camp in the farthest reaches of Siberia.

"What happened when you went to the office?"

"They had no birth record for Peter von Kraus. When I told them I was adopted, they said I needed to bring the papers so I could be registered properly because I wasn't a von Kraus or a Heinrich either," I said, referring to Greta and Ilse's birth surname.

"Pick a name."

"What?"

"Pick a name. I'll make sure you can get papers."

"How?"

"Ilya will make it happen."

"Your Russian lover?" Even I could hear the disdain in my voice.

"Don't judge, Peter. You were never one to judge. I am here alone. Many of the men my age are long dead from the war. I make Ilya cake and provide companionship and he makes sure I can get coal, that my house hasn't been repurposed by the state. That I can get paints from West Germany. My desires are few. My nights are no longer lonely in this big house."

"Cort." That came from Birgit.

Humiliation coursed through my veins. She'd fallen in love with the son of Viktor von Kraus. Not a Polish-German mutt of no proper lineage.

"I…" I didn't know what to say. How to fix what was irretrievably broken.

"Peter, I did not fall in love with your family name." She'd said that on the train, but even three hours ago it had seemed abstract. The documents between me and Greta made my status so much more precarious in a country where status meant everything.

"It's the reason you trusted me enough to invite me to your house," I said. A random apprentice without a hundred-year-plus family history may not have been invited to break bread by Birgit's father.

"Maybe," she admitted. "I can not say. But that boy I kissed was you. The boy I agreed to marry was you."

"Where is Cort from?" I asked. Things were going to change…again. I could either accept it or fight against it. Fighting never seemed to work for anyone.

"Brave. It's an old name that means brave."

"Peter?" Greta asked. It was startling how quickly things were changing. This morning I was Peter von Kraus. Next month, I'd be an entirely different person.

"Cort is fine. Pietrek Cort."

"Pietrek?" That was Greta.

"It's the Polish form of Peter," I said, though if pressed I couldn't say where that knowledge had come from. "It's the perfect compromise."

"Pietrek Cort. It's nice to meet you. Congratulations on your upcoming nuptials. Let's celebrate with cake." Greta did a big flounce, swished her long coat, and went for the silver cake knife, tarnish darkening its decorative handle.

"Everything is better with cake," Birgit said as she pulled plates from an open shelf.

Then we sat down, ate cake, and made plans.

15

"Where's your dad?" Lulu asked from her bed. She'd finally put away the BlackBerry that had commanded so much of her attention. I knew it was Sinclair and not Dalton Lacey, but I didn't see any point in continuing to chastise her for piling worse choices onto bad ones.

"Taking a walk," I answered. "A long walk."

"Is he going to be okay? Older people can get lost, you know."

"Maybe he'll remember enough Polish to get directions back to the hotel." I couldn't keep the snark from my response.

"You seem angry."

"I don't want to be." I unclenched my jaw to ease the ache there. "It's irrational..."

"But..."

"My last name isn't even my last name. My parents have kept this big secret for all these years. Why didn't they ever tell me any of this? It's not like they're not citizens or something. There were no repercussions from telling me the truth, except maybe me knowing who they really were…are."

"You know now."

"I don't even know what I'm going to say to my mother when we get home." I'd been mulling that one over in my mind since we'd left Bad Arolsen and the tracing service offices. Why had she kept my father's secrets?

"It wasn't her secret to tell," Lulu said in answer to my silent question.

"That's convenient."

The BlackBerry that Lulu had hidden somewhere on her person was ringing—again. What in the hell could she and Sinclair have to talk about? Or maybe I was the messed-up one. Maybe when people were truly compatible, they couldn't get enough of each other. I'd felt that way about exactly no one. I really thought loving with one's head had to be better than loving with one's heart. The heart was a liar.

Lulu looked around, embarrassed. Flustered.

I sighed. "Just get it."

"Hello," she said into the phone. The transformation of my best friend was fascinating. Her usually loud and strident voice softened as did her face. She smiled like she was lit from the inside.

"We've been kind of busy here. Yes…yes…I'll put you on speaker."

I could feel my eyebrows come together and my face squinch. "What?" I mouthed. Lulu's answering gesture was unintelligible. She pressed a few buttons, then Sinclair's voice came through the phone.

"Casey?"

"This is she," I answered with exaggerated formality.

"This is Richard Sinclair. How are you?"

How in the hell was I supposed to answer that? If Lulu wasn't going to be herself, I decided to take up the mantle.

"It's been a difficult trip. My father just saw his sister for the first time in sixty-four years. They don't even speak the same language anymore. How about you?"

"Wow. That had to be hard, but probably worth it to find that closure. It's exactly what I'm looking for myself. I'm pretty sure Lulu asked you about representing me."

"Professor Sinclair—"

"Call me Richard. We're all colleagues now. There's no power differential."

"Richard, Lulu did indeed mention that you were facing a divorce in the near future. I don't think, however, me representing you is a good idea. I am happy, however, to make a referral. I think you might be comfortable with Madeline Montgomery. She's got a great track record in Cuyahoga County. Gerald Popovic also comes to mind. He's a bulldog that anyone would be happy to have on their side."

"Why not you? Lulu says you're excellent."

"Why would you want me? There are better connected and more experienced lawyers in Cleveland."

"I just thought we'd work well together. That you'd be happy to return the favor."

"Favor?" I asked. The beauty of not sleeping with someone is that you didn't have to be solicitous.

"I represented you back when you were having your problems with the school. Maybe we were meant to be together during our difficult moments."

"Thanks so much for thinking of me. I don't think I'll be back in Domestic Relations for now. I'll be happy to have my secretary send over some referrals. I'll get your contact details from Lulu. It was nice talking to you. I'm going to step out of the room now so that you guys can have some privacy."

My dad was in his own room in this boutique Krakow hotel, and I was sharing a double with Lulu. Either way, the rooms in this early-century building, even with renovations, were tight quarters. There was no such thing as privacy while we were within the same four walls.

I closed the door behind me, careful not to make too much noise, and stepped in the quiet carpeted hall. I walked a few feet to my dad's room and knocked on the door, fully expecting him to still be outside walking and thinking, but surprisingly he pulled open the door. Haggard wasn't a flattering adjective, but it was the best one to describe my father.

I knew my dad was getting older. He'd passed all the milestones. Retirement, AARP magazines showing up in the mailbox, collecting social security. But for the first time, I was starting to see his age.

"Are you sixty-nine?" I asked, after I'd stepped into the room and took a seat on the too-small desk chair.

"They…the German orphanage officials…did change my birthday. Friedrich says it happened often, basically lowering ages to compensate for bed wetting or muteness. Younger children are more attractive."

"I learned that at Hudson. I knew you objected to me taking on the adoption work, but you never said why, so I ignored you. If you'd told me about any of this, you know I'd have listened, been more considerate of your opinion."

"Changed your mind?"

"I'm not sure, Dad. Maybe? Maybe not. I wouldn't have had any reason to believe that adoptions, especially at an agency like Hudson, were anything but above board."

"Giving one person's child to another, especially if that child can't speak for themselves, will always be open to corruption."

"I'm really sorry, Dad. I'm really sorry that this happened to you."

"It wasn't you, Casey. Poland was squeezed from two sides, the Nazis on one front, the Russians on the other. We didn't stand a chance."

"World War II fucked the world in so many ways. Excuse my—"

"That's exactly the right word, Casey. It took almost fifty years to sort it out...mostly. America prospered first. Then Japan. Then Europe finally put their differences behind them and formed the EU. Russia's finally been sidelined after wreaking a century of havoc. It mainly turned out okay."

"How do you want to leave it with your sister?"

"We're flying out Sunday."

"So?"

"My niece called. I'm going over on Saturday. Anna wants to take me to our mother's grave."

"Oh, Daddy. I'm sorry."

"If there's one thing I've learned, it's that you can't turn back time. You can't make a decision twice. Just once. Are you going to marry him, Casey?"

"Miles?"

"Has anyone else proposed to you? By my count, you're two for two. Tom Brody and this Miles Siegel."

"I don't...I don't know."

"Can I say something?"

"Sure."

"If it's not an enthusiastic yes, then the answer is no. I'm all for thinking about things. Weighing major life decisions, but not on love."

"He's good on paper. He went to an Ivy League school. He's an up-and-coming government prosecutor. He's well-off."

"You wouldn't be marrying his framed diploma or his money. You'd be marrying the man himself. And you didn't say one word about *him*."

"I'm afraid, Daddy."

"Afraid of what?"

"That no one will ever love me, like you love Mama."

"Oh, honey, why would you think that?"

"Because I'm going to be thirty-six in three days and I'm no closer to happily ever after than I was ten years ago—the last time I thought I had it all figured out."

"I love you more than life itself, honey. I promise you that there's a man out there who will love you like that. Who will worship the ground you walked on just because *you* walked on it."

"I wish he'd get here already. I don't want to be fifty before I meet him."

"There's so much we can't control about our lives. It's best to let love take care of itself."

"Says someone who met his true love at twenty-four."

I turned the three-stone ring around my finger once, then twice, before pulling it off and squeezing it in my palm as my fantasies of a perfect life with Miles drifted away like so much smoke.

16

I brushed leaves from the sparse grass and knelt at the gravesite. The tombstone was shiny, its crisp and neat engraving out of place among older, aged stones. It read, Maria Zamjoski, 1917-2006.

"Where is our father? Shouldn't their names be on a stone together?"

"His body is lost," Erika answered for Anna. "Let me think how to say this in English." She paused for a long, excruciating moment. "He is buried in a mass grave that was made along the roadside between Poland and Germany. He had to, probably, dig it himself. They did it like that during the war. After the hole was dug, they'd shoot half the people into it and make the remaining prisoners shovel the dirt back along top."

I didn't have any questions after that. After Anna had shown me the pictures from last night, I'd had so many vivid dreams of what I thought Poland was from when I was three or four. I hadn't mentioned them to anyone at breakfast in the hotel basement because I still wasn't sure if the dreams were real or just from my overactive imagination filling in gaps that I hadn't known were missing.

Anna knelt down next to me, fresh tears coursing down her cheeks. She touched my arm gently.

"You remember nothing of me?" she asked in halting English. She must have practiced the phrase just to speak it to me today.

I'd stood in the hot shower, staring at the intricate patterns of the Polish tiles thinking about this question I knew would come. I suspected the answer would be hard for her to hear, but I decided to speak it anyway. Even though my answer was in English, and it would be for Anna's daughter to translate, I looked directly in my sister's eyes that were so much like my own.

"When I was adopted to the von Kraus family, an older girl was taken in at the same time as me. She was Polish. My aunt said we spoke the language to each other for a time until we didn't anymore. Her name was also Anna. She neatly fitted into the sister space in my brain, I think. Maybe that. In America, they would say it was the trauma of the situation that altered my memory. I like to think, though, it was enough to have an older sister around. To have someone to make me feel safe. Keep me protected."

Anna said something in Polish. Her daughter said, "She is happy that you were not alone. Her greatest fear had always been that you were some scared little boy somewhere, the camps maybe, waiting for your death. She wants to know if you talk to the other Anna?"

I had to blink away my own tears then. In many ways, I was grateful that I'd been taken away…kidnapped, really, at such a young age.

The brain, I'd learned, is an amazing organ. It does an amazing job of protecting our psyches from traumatic memories in many cases.

The other Anna's brain wasn't so good at that, though. Maybe because she was older. Maybe because her own brain worked differently. She had been, in many ways, more damaged than me. She'd been kind of somber. Rarely talked unless someone had asked her a question. Stayed in her room most of the time. I'd tried a bunch of times to get her to go out with me on what Greta called her big adventures, but as often as she said yes, she also said no.

I mostly hadn't been surprised when Anna had taken Viktor's suggestion to work for a hat maker some distance away. She would get a trade and build the kind of solitary life she'd seemed to have wanted. After she hadn't responded to my first few letters, I'd given up. I regretted this now, so very much. Maybe I could have been a friend to her. Maybe I could have brought her to America. But as it stood, now, I knew as little about this second Anna as I did the first.

"I lost track of her when I went to America," I said.

"Mama would have been so happy that we have found each other," Anna's daughter translated. "You were her lost boy. She lit a candle for you every year on your birthday."

"Remember that year we were in Chicago and they were doing a whole Bastille Day celebration and I thought it was just for your birthday." It was the first thing Casey had said since we'd arrived at the cemetery.

"Bastille Day?"

"It's a French holiday. Celebrating revolutionaries storming the Bastille? I'm not sure, but it's cool to have a national holiday on Daddy's birthday."

"Is Bastille Day not in July?" Erika said, her eyes suddenly full of confusion.

"Of course. It's July fourteenth," Casey answered, sure of her facts as lawyers were.

A long look passed between Anna and Erika. Then rapid Polish passed back and forth between them.

"Your birthday was on the fourteenth, but in January," Erika finally said.

My Casey, who took nearly everything with grace, visibly paled.

"January? During the middle of the winter? Your birthday was always in the summer. Mama always complained about baking in the heat. Remember the hot summer in nineteen eighty-eight? The candles melted before Mama could light them." Casey turned to Erika. "Is your mom sure? January?"

There was a lot more Polish before Erika spoke.

"It was cold and dark. It snowed the day you were born. We had one of those huge heaters in the apartment. The ones that are nearly two meters tall and covered in green and white tiles. Papa made sure it was hot. So it was cold outside, but we were sweating in the apartment so that you wouldn't get cold. I'll never forget that, Marek...Pietrek...Peter." Erika stumbled over the last bit, naming me.

"Someone at the meeting did say something about shaving off months to make a younger child more attractive to adopting families," Casey supplied.

"I am sorry," Erika said. Whether it was her genuine expression of regret or Anna's, I didn't know. I was going to ask for clarification, but then realized it didn't make a difference either way. It was a sorry situation. One where the people at fault were all long dead.

"What's done is done," I said. Then I stood as quickly as my creaky knees would allow, which was not quick at all. I brushed off the twigs, a few stray leaves of grass. It was like Marek Zamojski was dead and buried in the ground with my mother. I don't know when it happened, but on that day in 1942, I think he ceased to exist. I was ready to go back to Peter Cort's life in Cleveland. I missed my wife. I wanted to be back in my kitchen with its old, too loud phone and the smell of baking. I wanted to wake up on West Boulevard where I knew there would be no surprises.

As we prepared for goodbye, Casey hugged her cousin and aunt. I hugged my sister and niece. They wished us a safe trip back to America. We promised to keep in touch. I could only breathe and relax once we were back in the car.

"You okay, Dad?" Casey asked while maneuvering through the winding streets.

"You need a new car."

"Probably should have bought a good used one and not spent my money on Arhaus furniture."

"You deserve both."

"I can't afford both."

"But I can. Let's go shopping on Tuesday. There are more sales at the end of the month. It'll be from us to you for your birthday."

"Dad, you don't have to do that."

"Tomorrow, all three of us are getting on an airplane and going back to the United States. Look at what happened to me during the war, what happened to so many people. We...all of us spend too much time thinking and stressing and worrying. I don't want you to worry. I don't want to worry about you in that ancient car. Seize the day and all that. No one knows about tomorrow."

"Will Mama be okay?"

"I'm sure she will be fine. I love you, my dear heart. I don't say this enough, but I love you. I'm grateful that I got to spend every night of your childhood under the same roof. I'm grateful for all the times we can spend together now. The last thing I want to worry about is you stranded on the side of some road in an old car because of your pride."

"Thank you."

"You are very welcome." Casey's safety was only a third of it. Another third was that I did want to give her something while I was still alive and could help her. But the last bit, the part that had motivated me was a bit of what Americans called "retail therapy."

Shopping for the car, I hoped, would help soothe her after she broke her second engagement. Obviously I was biased, but I thought my daughter was beautiful and smart and any man should be grateful to have her in his life.

The men of Cleveland didn't seem to agree. I didn't want her to have to wait any longer to have the things in life that she wanted and deserved. I was one man who would love her unconditionally, always. I vowed to show that bit to her more often. Maybe then she'd know what real love was like when it finally came her way.

17

"I need your keys," Sinclair said the moment he'd picked up his phone in answer.

He'd messaged me a bunch of times. It's one of the reasons I didn't go to the cemetery. So that I could answer his call in private. Without Casey looking down her nose at me while we talked. Also, a visit to the dead felt very much like a family thing where no one needed me intruding.

"What keys?" I asked. I didn't want to panic. But the palm holding my BlackBerry was sweaty, and my heart was speeding up, sure signs that the panic I didn't want to feel was about to settle in for a spell.

"To your place," Sinclair clarified.

"Why?"

"Deborah wants me out. She said by November first, but I'd like to get a jump on it. The situation here is tense, to say the least."

I love him. I love him. I love him.

I repeated this to myself three times, silently. Was I a horrible girlfriend if I didn't *want* to live with him? I mean, we'd talked about being together and getting married down the road, after he got the guts to tell his daughter about us and leave his wife. Part of me suspected that he'd never tell her. He'd been a placeholder until I found my guy, found my *real* relationship. Now, all of a sudden, this *was* my real relationship.

I wasn't ready.

"Tallulah? Did you hear me?"

"Yeah. Most of it. Polish cell service."

"You want this, right? You're the one who has been pushing for a commitment, something long term. I say let's do it."

For another long period of phone silence, I tried to re-member any conversation where I'd been pushing him. I couldn't bring even one to mind, but if he was saying it, I must have done it. Must have pushed it down somewhere deep in my subconscious right next to the shame of dating another woman's husband, no matter how fractured their relationship was.

"The only person who has keys is Casey," I lied. There was no way I was sending him to my parents' house. I'd want to postpone any more conversations about Sinclair as long as humanly possible once I landed back in Cleveland.

"And she's there with you."

"Yep, but we're flying back early tomorrow."

"When are you going to dump that bitch? She refused to take my case."

My mind scrambled to gain purchase. Had he just said what I thought I'd heard?

"Um...I can't believe you said that. You really shouldn't talk about her like that."

"Like what? Your so-called best friend is acting like a big old cunt. I did her a favor years ago. A big career-risking-type favor, and she can't even take my money."

"Sinclair! That's... Please don't use that word."

"What word?"

"That 'c' word."

A bark of laughter came through the speaker. I moved the phone away from my ear for a few seconds.

"You know I was joking, right?" he said through another laugh.

"It wasn't funny." *I* wasn't laughing.

"Oh my God. I can't take another woman with no sense of humor. I'm not mad at you or Casey. I get it. She's busy or whatever." Another hearty laugh came from Sinclair across thousands of miles of phone lines or whatever they used to transmit signals these days.

"That wasn't funny."

"Yes it was. I'm sorry if you can't take a joke."

"It wasn't kind."

"Tallulah has a limited sense of humor when it comes to her friends. Noted."

"Please don't make that kind of joke again."

"I don't know why you're making such a big deal about this. Let it go. We're going to move in together. No more nights apart. We'll have weekend mornings together in bed."

"You were kidding?"

"Oh my God. Yes. I really like your friend Casey. She's smart and driven. It's a lot more than I can say about some of the clowns you graduated with."

"If it was only a joke…" I hedged. Relented in my own unjustified anger.

"Yes. Now about moving in. You have a two-bedroom, right? I've never really been in that other room."

"It's storage, mostly. I was going to turn it into an office, but I already have one at work."

"Perfect. I'll need my own space. It can be a den. I'll bring over my desk. So should I schedule the movers for Halloween?"

"I may be jet-lagged," I said.

"You won't have to lift a finger. Not one. You can even take a nap. I'll just be bringing my clothes and a couple of pieces from the den. This is going to be great. I better get cracking."

"Sinclair. Wait. Before you hang up. Please no more slights about Casey."

"Got it. Point taken. I love you, okay? I know this is kind of sudden, but it's the right time for this. The right time for *us*. I can feel it in my bones. You won't regret it. Okay? I can schedule the movers?"

"Yes. It'll be good, right? It'll be us."

"Good girl. Safe flight. Call me the minute you land and when you're back in your apartment. That's two calls, okay? Try not to forget. I don't want to have to worry about you."

I promised to make both of those calls. Then I punched the button to end the call, but Sinclair had already disconnected.

18

"How was your first trip to Europe? I can't believe you'd never been abroad before. I loved Krakow when I was a little kid," Miles said. He pronounced the city name like he was a native. That little bit of class difference, the one we never talked about, made my belly twinge. He was deep in reminiscence and didn't notice my discomfort. "We walked all the way across town to Wawel castle. I remember that Mom wanted to see the interior. She loves all those antiques and wall hangings. But I was a kid, so I got my way. We did some tour of the armory instead. Lots of weapons everywhere."

"I'm sure your mom loved that." I tried to keep my sarcasm light.

"I think she did." It was so light it went straight over his head. Smiling broadly, he continued, "She likes to see me happy and have new experiences. She bought me a gelato afterwards. I remember that being good."

"The trip was harder than I thought it would be," I admitted after a long moment of silence between us.

"I can only imagine." Miles, who was leaning his butt against my windowsill, looked at his designer watch. I glanced down at my own simple timepiece, another sharp contrast. Miles had pointed out months ago how much we had in common, and all that about our education and upbringing had been true. Lately though, the differences seemed like a yawning chasm. "You want to skip out and grab a drink, maybe dinner? I've had some thoughts about places we can go now that you have a passport."

"That passport book didn't come with a passbook savings account attached. I'm still pretty strapped until I figure out how I'm going to hustle up new clients," I said. Five years ago I'd have made up a different excuse, but I was tired of pretending to be things I wasn't, namely secure in my job, or always successful at it.

"I'll pay, Casey," Miles said, like his largesse was the most obvious solution to my poverty problem. "Of course I don't expect you to foot the bill. Not for business class tickets or a four-star hotel. It's not the only way to travel, but it is more comfortable."

"Not coach?"

"I've never done it. There's no nobility in flying in the back. My parents have been more than generous. You'll be family soon. I'm happy to share this part of my life with you."

My stomach decided at precisely that moment to rumble like an unwanted guest.

"You *are* hungry. C'mon. It's Friday. You'll still need to figure out what direction you want to go on Monday. You'll have had a weekend of proper sleep and nourishment."

"I haven't eaten all day," I mumbled, avoiding what I needed to do. Needed to say. "That's why it's making that noise."

"Why haven't you eaten anything?" Before I could get a word in, he was speaking again. "Must be jet lag. You have to get out in the sun and get back to your rhythms even if you don't feel like it."

"I didn't eat because I was too nervous about seeing you," I blurted out.

"Nervous?"

I took a deep breath, two. Tried to swallow down my fear.

"I'm not ready to get married." Even though I'd gone to a near whisper, Miles heard me loud and clear.

"You need the big party, huh? I thought that might be the case. No Gibraltar elopement, then."

He leaned a little more on the sill. Kicked out his chukka-clad feet farther into my office.

"It's not because I want a reception with hundreds of people…" Though that's exactly what I did want…eventually. It was just that the family on the other side of the aisle was no longer the large, influential Brody clan, or the quietly rich Siegel nuclear family. It was some as yet unknown group of people who would become my extended family. "It's because I'm not ready to get married."

It took a minute, but I saw the moment that Miles cottoned on to what I was afraid to voice, to articulate out loud.

"It's not that you don't want to get married now," he concluded. His own voice was a near whisper of rejection. "It's that you don't want to get married to me."

"You're a great guy, Miles." When he looked like he was going to say something, I rushed on filling that small gap of silence with more. "I'm just in a state of flux right now. There are so many things in my life that are unsettled."

"You can't wait until you're ready. That's true for everything, not just marriage, but kids, career change. No one is ever ready."

"I don't love you like I need to—to marry you. I love the idea of you. A..." I hesitated, extracted the word "rich" from my impromptu speech, then soldiered on, "...guy who can sweep me off my feet. It's just that we're too different."

"Is this about race? Is my being black or biracial or half Jewish the part that makes me too different?"

"No. Miles." My voice was loud and matter-of-fact. "That's not it. That'll never be it. I've been running around for nearly ten years looking to be saved. I thought the Brodys would save me. I thought you would save me. The only person who can save me...is me. I need to be my own biggest cheerleader."

"I'd support you."

"I think I want something different out of love. I was looking to fill a hole with marriage. While I was driving all around Poland and Germany, I realized I want that fluttering-stomach, erratic-heartbeat, can't-get-enough-of-each-other love. I think we can agree that we don't have that."

"You sound like the back cover of a romance novel. We get along. We're compatible in and out of bed. That's more than most people get. It's what my parents had."

"They're getting a divorce, Miles. I'd say that kind of marriage comes with an expiration date."

"Touché."

"I want what my parents have, a true romantic partnership."

He looked skeptical. "Still?"

"Still. I may not get that, but I'm unwilling to settle. You should be too, not willing to settle that is."

"So that's it?"

"I don't want to break up a third time. So yes, I think we need to call it quits once and for all."

"You sound so clinical."

"Miles, please. Don't make this hard. I love you. I just don't see a future that I want if we continue down this path—"

The phone bleated, filling the room with its urgent sound.

"Where's everybody?" He gestured toward the empty office that was next to mine, the empty reception area.

"It's after five on a Friday. I'll have to get this. It may be some kind of client emergency."

"Casey Cort." I made my voice very adult and official.

"Casey Cort? It's Dion Fortune." Of all the people I thought may be calling my work phone, Dion Fortune had been last on that list.

That blast from the not-so-distant past nearly knocked me off my feet. "I can't talk right now. I have someone in my office."

"It's about the business. It's about Intraport."

"Now is not a good time." I tried to squeeze all the meaning I could into those five words. I wanted my client to hear that his prosecutor was in the room with me and hadn't stopped gunning for him some two years later.

"But..." Dion's impatience came through the receiver loud and clear.

"I'll have to call you back," I insisted.

"It's urgent."

"Give me a few..."

The call abruptly disconnected. I looked at the phone. Put it down. Turned my attention back to Miles.

"Who was that?"

I couldn't tell him that it was the missing puzzle piece from the biggest case he'd lost. So I gave the only appropriate answer.

"Attorney-client privilege. I'm sorry, but I have to go. It does look like it's going to be some kind of emergency. I'll get the ring back to you. Jet lag is worse than I thought it would be, and I forgot to put it in my bag before I came downtown. Can't think too well tired."

Miles looked at me like I was some sad stray puppy, not devastated—like a woman had just broken his heart. That look alone firmed up my convictions that I'd done the right thing.

"Please keep it," he offered. "It was special to you. There's nothing to be done with it at this point."

"Okay. Fine. Thanks. So..."

"Are you sure about this? If I walk out that door, I don't think I'll ever be coming back."

"I understand, Miles. I really do. It's a small town. I know we'll run into each other, so let's agree to be friends." I went in for the hug and bumped into his hand which was extended for a shake. If that wasn't embarrassing enough, my phone rang again. I knew it was my old client calling back.

It was as if the ringtone itself sounded more urgent with each passing ring.

"Sorry," I said. I shook the proffered hand, then he used that grip to pull me in for a hug. We stood that way for a long time, holding each other. I tried not to cry while the phone continued bleating. Finally, it once again went silent. Crying would be for later when I was home with Simba on my lap and a fork in my hand digging into whatever my mother had sent my way in the foil-topped pan I'd jammed into the fridge.

I was sad, very sad because I was giving up the possibility of something almost like happily ever after for the vast unknown. A world where I may never find the love of my life. If there was one thing I knew, it was that whatever I had with Miles would have been fine. Maybe good enough, even. Something about that brief time in Poland and Germany let me know that fine wasn't going to be enough.

Not anymore.

I showed Miles out the door. It was past five and my secretary, Letty, and our shared receptionist were long gone. For my own peace of mind, I locked the door to the office suite behind him. I wanted to review some files and get ready to jump back into work on Monday morning.

The phone rang one last time. I ran back through the small waiting area to my office and picked up the phone again.

"Casey Cort," I said to the voice on the other end. "I can talk to you now. The coast is clear."

ABOUT THE AUTHOR

Aime Austin is the author of the Casey Cort Legal Thriller Series. Casey is almost always in trouble. Aime's full time job? Rescuing her. Good thing Aime's got experience. She practiced family and criminal law in Cleveland, Ohio for several years—so she has the skills for the job.

When Aime isn't rescuing Casey from herself, she's raising her son or traveling between Budapest and Los Angeles.